Kirstie Speke was born in 1971. She lives in East London with her husband. Previously she has been a fashion stylist and a night-club promoter. She has also lived in New York and Los Angeles.

Angel is her first novel. It was shortlisted for the Eastside Novelists' Award.

ANGEL

KIRSTIE SPEKE

PIATKUS

For more information on other books
published by Piatkus, visit our website at
www.piatkus.co.uk

Copyright © 2001 by Kirstie Speke

First published in Great Britain in 2001 by
Judy Piatkus (Publishers) Ltd of
5 Windmill Street, London W1T 2JA
email:info@piatkus.co.uk

The moral right of the author has been asserted

A catalogue record for this book is available from the British Library

ISBN 0 7499 3252 X

Set in Perpetua by Palimpsest Book Production Limited,
Polmont, Stirlingshire
Printed and bound in Great Britain by
Cox & Wyman Ltd, Reading, Berkshire

Dedicated to the memory of Mary Christine Speke,
my brave and beautiful mother.

CHAPTER 1

My father gave me the name Uma – a Hindu goddess, a bestower of blessings. It was his parting gift before he bolted back to Bombay and pleased his parents with a more suitable match. He is the reason my skin is golden like honey and turns reddish brown in the sun; my colouring is the envy of my mother with her cod-belly white legs. My father is also responsible for my hair, which is wild, black and wavy and hangs down my back in thick coils.

The last of his gifts, as far as I am aware, are my short-sighted, dark eyes. The images I see are soft and blurred, like wedding photographs with everything bathed in a gentle haze. I am still bull-headed enough to refuse to correct my sight, however, I concede to a pair of thick, heavy glasses which I wear only under the camouflage of darkness in the cinema. I prefer my own soft focus world; I'm happy not to see the cracks. I like to look in the mirror and see my own features reflected gently, like a Disney version of myself. My father also wore thick glasses. My mother mentioned this only once, then she snapped shut and looked annoyed, as if I had tricked her into revealing more than she wished.

I learned how I came to be through my favourite childhood pursuit of spying. I used to pretend to be fast asleep at my grandmother's house, curled up in her chair, perfectly still, breathing as slowly as I could. I would sit as motionless as the brass monkeys on her mantelpiece, listening to the steady beat of my feigned sleep and words not destined for my little ears. I am still not averse to hiding and peeping in places that I shouldn't.

I was a fairly contented child, but every summer I would wish for a sister. I would blow on the fluffy, white balls of dandelion seeds and watch the 'fairies' that carried my wish fly over the back fence. My second wish, the one I reserved for the final blast of breath necessary to get those last stubborn seeds airborne, was to have hair as blonde and straight as the girls who were chosen to be angels in the school play. I would stand clutching the exhausted stalk and silently long for my hair to shine yellow in the sun. I have long since lost my desire for Barbie locks and all that it signified to me then, but I never lost the wish carried on that first hopeful puff of breath.

Now I am twenty-seven years old and lucky enough to own a small patch of lawn which is riddled with long, green stalks topped with white afros graciously swaying in the wind, I realise I have run out of wishes. I have reached a stage of absolute suspension, hung like a comic book spider frightened to swing backwards or forwards in case the thread breaks.

Home is two storeys of blackened bricks that make up my East End terrace, which is perched in the middle of a winding road in Whitechapel. The houses are all early Victorian, and late at night there is a Jack the Ripper chill to the empty streets. The days are quite different. There are young children everywhere, playing in the gardens and spilling on to the pavement. There is the market a few streets away, where there is the constant movement of people, produce, cheap clothes and polyester saris flapping in the wind, and spiked jack fruits like sleeping armadillos stacked high outside the shops. It is where veteran old dears with breeze-proof cauliflower perms gossip viciously about their neighbours: 'Thinks she's bloody Joan Collins she does – sequins at her age!'; teenage girls deliberate over skimpy tops in pastel lycra, and dark-eyed women in black headscarves, impervious to the sales banter of the Cockney barrow boys, wheel their plump, sleeping babies along the busy High Street.

This summer I have not been to the market or to any other lively place. Instead I've pottered between house and garden with black feet and bare legs. I've managed to maroon myself, and despite the fixed nature of these crumbling bricks there is a perfect feeling of being adrift. I could be anywhere – or perhaps, more accurately, nowhere at all.

It has been eight weeks since I watched, over the top of a tabloid, my husband box up his things and leave. It was a strange day for him to choose to finish the marriage. For us,

Sunday was a day of newspapers and sex; Saturday was the day for rows and fury. I watched him blankly and marvelled at how little he had accumulated over the past four years. The clutter and chaos I had presumed was joint turned out to be mostly mine. The only really noticeable void is in my bed. My husband's ghost still seems to occupy the left-hand side. Sometimes in the haze of early morning I expect to feel the gentle squish of warm testicles until I wake up properly and remember he has left and taken all his body parts with him.

I am lucky in that I have been left geographically unmoved by this new twist of fate. I can keep my castle and he can take his box of tricks and set them up elsewhere. We were like two unrelated, ferocious creatures in a small box. Now we really should have less need to fight so dirty. I can remove my paws from his eyes, he can remove his teeth from my tail and we can both scamper off quite merrily.

For my part, I have run to a glorious state of self-exile and unleashed the misanthropic hermit I never allowed myself the luxury to become. My reclusive state was wonderfully easy to achieve; I simply unplugged the phone and left the door unanswered, which allows me to run about house and garden with banshee hair and dark-circled panda eyes and remain undisturbed. I have always known that without the influence of outside civilization I would soon resort to looking like a mad woman. On my occasional trips for food and wine I have to check myself in the mirror to make sure I won't frighten anyone. Without having looked at my reflection for a while, I'm never quite sure what my face, or

4

the rebellious overgrown thatch of black curls on my head, will be up to. I was always far more inclined to run to seed than appear cultivated. In no time at all I'm as raggedy as the weeds that rule over my patch of lawn. Living in this casual, solitary fashion means that time seems to flow very fast indeed, with very little to distinguish one day from the next. Sleeping and eating are the only real milestones.

There was a problem that threatened my solitude. As I am now a household of one, all the bills that arrive belong solely to me. In two months I had filled a whole toast rack with them. This state of affairs coincided with the fact that some of the people in the offices of the various publications I work for have spotted that the pictures they commission me to draw have begun to bear no resemblance to the piece they should illustrate. It has taken them quite a while to notice. I suppose all this time they have imagined I've been making some very clever illustrative pun that they were not smart enough to decipher. Some bright spark (probably a junior who is less hardened to nonsense) has now noticed and I have seen a gradual drying up of work. They are punishing me for their earlier indulgence and I am left with enough work to either house me or feed me, but not both.

The only option that allowed me to remain sequestered was to rent out the one room in the house that has been left, by dint of my new single status, relatively empty. It used to house grey suits, multi-coloured ties and boxes of painfully bad records from the Eighties, but these were male things, and it was now cleansed of such and fit for human habitation. It was large enough and empty enough to rent out – the challenge was to find someone who would not disturb the tranquil vacuum that had successfully bred in my house; someone who would not try and befriend me and mix up our lives in some big, jolly, communal pot. I had a notion of a pale wisp of a person, our communication limited to a series of polite smiles on the rare times we encountered each other. I could just about handle that. I came up with some words that I hoped conveyed the right message:

Tenant wanted E1
One room in house
Shared facilities
Self-contained attitude
Occupation irrelevant

The advert looked sullen when I saw it in print, but it was to the point and matched my mood. I received two replies, which I screened through my newly reinstated answering machine. One was from a foreign man; I could not locate the accent. He left a stream of intimate details, as if he had perhaps mixed up my number with another from the personal column. The other reply was reassuringly curt, from a woman with a strong, low voice and faint northern burr. Her tone was sharp – it was not a voice for confidences over the kitchen table. I was pleased to hear the clicking in of a message tape when I phoned back so I could discharge the task without having to speak to her directly.

Then I spent two hours placing my disorder into small stacks, which improved the immediate impression of the general state of things. Tidying myself took less time. I scraped my Medusa locks into a thick plait and painted out the black circles under my eyes. I even chose some smartish clothes and roughly co-ordinated them in an attempt to make a reasonable impression. Lately my neighbours had been treated to the sight of me wandering the back garden in nothing but saggy-arsed shorts and faded, shapeless tee-shirts.

She arrived well after I had been lulled into thinking nobody would show up and had relaxed a little. The bell made me jump. I stood at the doorstop blinking up at her. The sun bounced off her huge hair, which was streaked with bold stripes of gold and blonde. A Versace scarf looped around her neck. She was far too glamorous to be standing outside an East End terrace; it was as if she had been superimposed upon the scene. She towered above me like a Vegas billboard come to life. I felt like a very small beetle looking up at her, a black fuzz of wayward curls escaping from my plait. She looked about my age, but I couldn't imagine that we'd have anything else in common. It transpired that her name was not Angela, as I had thought, but the much more fitting and theatrical Angel. I would never have replied to her message if I'd realised her name was Angel; that in itself would have been enough to scare me off.

She followed me as I gave her a whistle-stop tour of my home, her face stuck in an amused, cynical expression, and dark sunglasses on the whole time. Taking her round I was struck by the fact that every room seemed to have shrunk and become more dated and slovenly than I'd realised.

'Fine, I'll take it. My things are outside in the cab,' she growled in a husky voice that made my surprised response sound like a squeak. I stood for a moment with a look of total uncomprehension on my face. She had come out with precisely the opposite announcement to the one I had been certain would follow our brief trip around my house.

I had found myself a tenant quicker than expected; someone who was a great deal more than a wisp. My short-sighted plans hadn't prepared me for the actuality of this, so I found myself lost for the words needed to wriggle out of it politely. I would have felt too foolish having to explain that I didn't really want anyone with a life living with me.

Within minutes I found myself unloading what seemed to be an unlimited supply of different shaped suitcases and vanity boxes from a black cab parked alongside a stony-faced driver. Angel carried a malevolent-looking, long-haired cat and one small, silver, circular case.

I felt the first serious wave of panic when the unloading finally came to an end and the cab driver, with an air of sadistic glee, left the remaining four boxes on the roadside and pulled off sharply. It was slowly sinking in that I had a flamboyant stranger with an enormous wardrobe and a funky smelling, fluffy cat to deal with. I dragged the remaining four boxes inside, still with that same vacuous look of shock on my face.

Angel was popping open a bottle of champagne in the

kitchen. I felt as though I had been picked up by a tornado, Wizard of Oz-style, and transported to another world. I accepted a glass of champagne in what looked like a mediaeval goblet and toasted the arrangement with my newly acquired housemate.

This was to be a stop gap we decided. Angel had only this afternoon left the 'lying, cheating, filthy bastard' she had been sharing a flat and a bed with. She would rent my room until she found somewhere more suitable. I felt duty bound to stay with her and continue her toasts; champagne is not a drink that should ever be drunk alone and Angel seemed to want to celebrate her arrival.

The opening of a second bottle kept me from scuttling to my room. But it was no longer simply compassion that stopped me from leaving her to settle in on her own. I was slightly drunk, a galaxy of tiny exploding bubbles attacking my empty stomach.

There were boxes piled either side of her with the heads of strange, Balinese wooden animals poking out from them and a real, flat-faced cat running around my ankles. Angel, I was pleased to see, was slightly more drunk than I was. I suspected she had had a head start. She was still occasionally chanting her original mantra of 'Bastard, Bastard, Bastard', which had started up when she first attempted to explain her hasty uprooting from Bayswater, although the subject soon skipped on to the urgent need for redecoration of my house and some ideas on how to introduce a Mexican theme to the kitchen.

The rest of the evening is a blur. The last thing I clearly remember was discovering the remnants of a bottle of whisky lurking in the back of the cupboard under the sink.

CHAPTER 2

When I regain consciousness, late the following morning, I have a very sore head and a pile of twenty-pound notes beside my bed. This is confusing at first, until it floats into my memory that I am no longer the sole occupant of this house and I have a month's rent on my bedside table. It is strange for me to have to face anyone in the morning. There is almost the embarrassment of a one-night stand when I go down to the kitchen; a general feeling of rash, drunken arrangements. There is no sign of Angel but there is sufficient evidence of her arrival. In every corner her presence is reflected in one way or another, from overfilled ashtrays to long, white cat hairs.

Angel wakes some time in the afternoon. By then, despite feeling nauseous, I have regained some composure and a vague grasp of the notion that I am the owner of this house. She comes down in full make-up with her hair pinned in two Danish pastry-type whirls either side of her head. I have a scrubbed, grey face among a wild tangle of hair. We both look at each other, momentarily alarmed.

'Good morning,' I manage, feeling and looking a lot sicker than Angel.

'You look like you need my very own hangover cure,' she says sweetly in her chain-smoker's voice, taking an enormous copper pan from one of the many boxes that have invaded my kitchen. She makes up a pan of fried eggs, and pours out two Bloody Marys using some miniature bottles of vodka she produces like magic from another box. I sit like a sick puppy and watch.

The combination works. The worst of my symptoms seem to be relieved a little; I am not quite up to direct sunlight yet but I am no longer flinching at daylight, and the slight green tinge has gone from around my gills. My gratitude is marred only by the memory that it was the arrival of Angel that brought on the excessive drinking that caused my sickness in the first place.

It is clear from Angel's dressing gown and Princess Leia hairstyle that she is not rushing to work today. My plans for an unobtrusive housemate have gone spectacularly awry right from the start. I suspect that Angel is also hoping that once I have been revived I might get dressed and trot off out to gainful employment. We are both going to be disappointed.

My apple-cart has been firmly upturned and there isn't even any point in scrabbling around to pick up the bruised remains. I am forced to sit at my desk and sketch pictures of commissions that I am unlikely to ever receive, in an attempt to ward off further friendliness. Angel fetches a pair of stylish, black sunglasses and suns herself in the backyard. I have always felt lucky to have a garden in London – all thirty-three feet of weed-infested grass, rocks and broken pots – and I suspect that Angel's presence in my humble home has more to do with the tanning potential of my west-facing backyard than anything else. It is not long before she provokes a sudden interest in horticulture from my neighbour Haroun.

Haroun is standing in the garden of his father's house where he plays at being landlord. He is loitering near the fence with an empty watering can, trying to elicit a response to his good-looks and big, brown cow eyes. He is still perplexed that his obvious physical charms have not seemed to disarm me yet. I am sure he has become accustomed to a slight flutter of excitement, a certain frisson in the air around unattached women under sixty. He is handsome, with smooth, round, girlish cheeks and wide, pouting lips. He is how I imagine a Hindu god, and I can picture a frame of light around his pretty face. I have taken great pleasure in steadfastly pretending not to have noticed his appeal. This is like sticking pins into his enormous bubble of vanity and it worries him. It has made him try even harder: the casual flick of the fringe; the disarming smile, like some discarded cheerleader desperate for attention. I have remained so calmly oblivious it has been driving him mad. If I had only once gazed dreamily over the back fence then he could have moved on to flirt with some other sad-faced girl, a silent victory registered. His intentions are quite harmless but I have thoroughly enjoyed the cruel pleasure of thwarting his vanity.

He seems very chirpy now he has spied Angel. She looks at him over the top of her fake Chanel glasses, one eyebrow cocked slightly higher than the other. I am still pretending to draw on the kitchen table but cannot help but peep through the plants on the window sill and listen out for their conversation. There is not a lot being said, and it is a very one-sided encounter; Angel simply throws the same quizzical look she was wearing when she first turned up here and Haroun flees. Knowing his ego-driven resolve I am surprised he didn't show a little more persistence. Later I try out that look of hers in the mirror. It doesn't work so well on me – I look like an angry ant.

Angel stays in the garden for the rest of the day, moving right to the very back section to get every last bit of the sun. She sits on top of a pile of rocks in between some sad, spikeless cacti, which were here when I moved in and look increasingly pitiful every year. The constant 'diddly-dee' of her mobile phone punctuates the silence. I grow restless sitting inside. I would like to go and sit in the sun; the air that breezes in through the back door has that wonderful aroma that is characteristic of these streets in summer. It is a potent mixture of spices, sun and smog. The smell is like an enormous exotic sponge cake just out of the oven. It is difficult to want to stay indoors when there is only one last strip of sunshine left and the air smells so sweet.

We sit in a prickly silence either side of a cacti. Angel has a full face of make-up on, which even with my poor sight I can see melting slightly in the sun. There is still the insistent buzz of the mobile but she coolly ignores it. We are a strange pair. Angel seems larger than life, and as I have been somewhat smaller than life these last two months we are spectacularly mismatched to share a house. Yet as we sit in silence I realise that I like Angel; she frightens me but I like her.

CHAPTER 3

Without intending to, I find myself enjoying the company of my new tenant. It seemed unreal at first, this big, blonde presence in my house, but in some strange way it works well. Angel has her own eccentric behaviour – what she calls 'people aversion', a condition that keeps her away from the hoi polloi and inside a little glamour bubble she's created for herself. She would be more likely to streak naked down the High Street than use the Underground. The last time she went to the cinema she saw *Blue Lagoon* (that was way back when Brooke Shields was still a virgin).

Angel claims that just the thought of public transport brings her out in hives. If she goes anywhere at all she needs to be driven. I don't think she would even post a letter without calling for a cab. She has a few select places that she will go to in times of excess cash when she needs to shop for clothes or other gorgeous things. Other than that her stomping ground tends to be the bars and nightclubs of the West End. Like myself, Angel doesn't go out very much in the daytime, so the two of us are stuck side by side in our separate worlds, and prompted by the compact nature of the space we share, our two lives start to coalesce more than I would have imagined.

She is obviously a lot more glamorous a recluse than I am, but then she's only cloistered until after dark; I'm more of a full-time hermit. A large proportion of her daytime hours are spent in the beautification process. I only use the mirror to check whether I have left any toothpaste in a rabid froth around my mouth. She will spend hours in the bathroom and come out with a cinematically perfect look. Then she will change four more times before she goes out for the evening. By the time she's ready to leave she looks as if she's casually popping off to collect an Oscar or two.

Glamorous as she is, she is not as grand as I first thought, however. She loves limousines, champagne and anything that *looks* expensive (she hates inconspicious consumption with a vengeance; Prada puts her in a rage – 'all that money to look like a kinky librarian!'), but she still cooks with lard. She was horrified when she caught me about to take a dress to the dry cleaner's and taught me the curative wonders of a damp rag and a big squirt of Chanel no. 5.

When she moved in I was worried that I might have to break my more slatternly habits and keep the place clean. But it turns out that neither Angel nor her cat are that fastidious. I remember her great pleasure in discovering a pair of false eyelashes she thought were lost for good. She found them nestling safely in the inch-thick scum on top of a forgotten cup of coffee that was hiding under the debris of discarded clothes in her room. We both have a very relaxed attitude to domestic chores, which helps seal our relationship as co-habitees.

What I like most about my unlikely housemate is that she makes me laugh. Even when I start off grouchy in one corner of the room with my sketch pad, she has a sneaky way of invading my quiet with her highly appealing brand of wickedness.

'Uma.'

'Mmm?'

'Is *this* what you were married to?' Somehow she has got her mitts on photographic evidence of the previous existence that I'd been trying to forget all about.

'I'm afraid so.'

'You ought to be ashamed of yourself! I hope you've changed the locks . . . I don't want to be surprised by *that* coming in the door one day. He looks just like one of those presenters on the Open University programmes they show at four in the morning. The sort that don't even look passable when you're just back from a club and really off your trolley. Next time, girlfriend, make sure you take a good look with your specs on before you go waltzing down the aisle.'

I can't escape her; there is something infectious about Angel's verbal mischief that lures me into being her audience whether I want to or not. From the very first evening when I listened to an hilariously unkind tirade against her ex-lover and some of his most personal details, I am reminded of the

19

fact that, having removed people from my life, there is a marked absence of laughter. Luckily I hadn't reached the stage where I would sit and cackle at my own private jokes, but it is reassuring when my seal-like yap of a laugh tumbles out again when put to the test by Angel. I seem to have gone from peaceful solitude to having a one-woman cabaret act in my house and I can't claim to dislike her jaded humour.

What impresses me most is her sheer Scarlett O'Hara verve – she views everything with a determined one-sidedness. On top of that she simply doesn't give a damn. People, or indeed anything at all, can be dismissed in an instant merely by a sharp change in her facial expression; or damned by the casual mutter of 'whatever'. I have never met anyone who defends themselves and their opinions, however outrageous, quite so pugnaciously or as humorously as Angel. She once spent a good half hour carefully explaining to me exactly why people who like marmalade are sick and twisted (I'm not keen on it myself but I still think her reasoning was a little harsh).

She has a very different way of dealing with things than I have: I lie down and play dead whereas Angel exorcises her demons by verbally flaying her ex-lover at every opportunity, constantly planning other more devious means by which to do damage to him. Her method seems a lot quicker than mine as she's already scanning the Lonely Hearts section in *Loot*.

'You of all people can't seriously be looking in there,' I say, amazed by her unlikely choice.

'Why not? I've found a couple this way.'

'But *Loot*'s for old washing machines and stuff like that.'

'Men, broken down washing machines – what's the big difference? Let me find you a nice one. Here you are – "Adventurous broadminded man looking for clean adult afternoon fun".'

'No, thank you.'

'We could always get him round for a bit of hoovering and dusting. This place could do with it. Ring it and say you thought it said "cleaning adult fun". Go on. I bet you're not as good as you pretend to be, anyway. Your husband's been gone for ages – you must be gagging for it by now. I'd be going up the walls if I'd been on my own for as long as you have.'

'I'm coping. I am not frustrated enough to invite strange men from classified ads round for an afternoon. They're probably all perverts.'

'So? As long as they're good-looking perverts with nice bodies, who cares? You're not waiting for that husband of yours to remember his way home, are you? I bet he's not wasting his time. It won't be long before he gets lucky and finds someone else with poor vision.'

'No, I'm not waiting for him to come back, but he's really not the type to be up to anything. He's not exactly Casanova. The silly sod just "needs some space to work on some personal issues". I don't know what the hell he meant by that but it's fine by me, just as long as he doesn't expect to come strolling back into my life.' He'd had the good sense to take most of his stuff with him. I suppose he realised there was a good chance that I might lug the whole lot to a car

21

boot sale and sell off his precious designer belongings at ten pence a throw. 'At the moment I really have no need for him or any of the betesticled species, thank you,' I say, hoping to put an end to the topic.

Angel gives me that half smile that sits on only one side of her face. I'm still not sure exactly what that look means. Whatever it means I am not ready to be launched as a singleton just yet. Though she is not entirely wrong when she says that I'm not as good as I make out. There are days when the sun shines and thoughts of sex flicker into my mind and have to be chased off. I think of work and bills, or the sight of the backs of my thighs in direct sunlight, in an attempt to banish that hungry feeling that has nothing to do with food.

CHAPTER 4

We have shared a space for three weeks, during which time I have never once seen Angel without a beautifully painted face. She looks fabulous, like a blonde Ava Gardner, but I am curious to know what's underneath. It's disconcerting when only a short while ago I was free to roam about my house as dishevelled as I wished, and so I'm making a little more effort in an attempt to lessen the vast disparity in our appearance.

It is Angel's feet that lead me to solve the mystery. I have neat feet. They are, I think, my best feature, providing they are clean and fragrant. Angel has really big, ugly feet; I even think I spotted what looked like dark stubble on her big toes. I have spent most of this summer in a pair of plastic flip-flops, which does not go unnoticed.

'You can't walk around in those.'

'I'm only in the garden,' I offer lamely.

'Even in the garden,' Angel says, finishing off the rest of

what she wants to say by moving her eyebrows slightly. I'm discovering that Angel's eyebrows have a larger vocabulary than most people. Arguments can be quashed just by a tilt of a well-plucked brow.

I find myself coerced into a mini-cab and taken to some strange shop in north London. In the window is a bizarre collection of glam-rock-type boots. Inside are more elegant spiky creations in leather and satin. Leopard-print, thigh-high boots with heels that look more like hooves sit beside Cinderella shoes in clear plastic set with iridescent beads. They are fantastical shoes, wonderful for women who don't take public transport or have to dodge kerb crawlers along Whitechapel High Street as they wend their way home late at night.

Behind the scenes it is an old-fashioned place, with a Dickensian-type workshop that is accessible from the back of the shop. This is full of grey-haired men busily working behind what look like oversized, black sewing machines; between each row of benches are mountains of scraps of multi-coloured leather and suede. There is a man in a smart suit, his trousers neatly rolled up to just below his knee, trying on a pair of gold slingbacks, elegantly sashaying back and forth in front of a small square mirror.

Angel is searching through the display for a size ten. But something has suddenly snapped into place, the possibility of which leaves me with a cartoon-style dropped jaw but does seem to make perfect sense. Some light-hearted remarks of Angel's that I just couldn't understand at the time pop into my head and become a whole lot clearer. The man in heels has not shocked me particularly – he did have nice enough ankles to carry off those shoes – but a penny has dropped. I look down at Angel trying to stuff her ugly sister-style feet into a pair of size nines. I notice she also has huge hands with big, round fingers. Hands and feet, I have since learned from Angel, are the great give-away.

I am too busy digesting my latest thoughts to pay much attention to the shop, despite chivvying from Angel to buy myself some sexier footwear. I leave her to wrestle a discount out of a grumpy-looking old man in a white overall and wait outside for her. We stop in a café and I seize my moment.

'Angel, when you said . . . umm, did you mean . . . were you—'

'A man?' She booms it out as an interruption to my dithering. Two old ladies sitting near the door turn round to stare at us with interest. 'You didn't know? I wasn't sure whether you'd clicked or not. You never noticed the occasional five o'clock shadow?'

'No.' I shake my head sheepishly, feeling more acutely than ever that reality can be very slippery sometimes.

'Blind bat!' Angel starts to laugh – a mad cackle that normally only surfaces when she is drunk, but my face, which is bug-eyed with shock, has sent her into this fit of hilarity.

We leave the café without saying much. I keep looking at her in disbelief, trying to make out her past gender in her face, but it is not easy to find there. It's hard for me to look at Angel in a different way; she is, if anything, far more feminine than I am. I can't help feeling foolish and a little alarmed. I have had enough changes of late.

Angel doesn't think it's a good idea for us to go home just yet. She claims that I am in need of an alcoholic revival to help me get over the shock. I'm not so sure, but Angel is adamant and drags me to one of the local pubs. It is not somewhere she'd normally be found but on this occasion she decides it will do. Thankfully, this particular public house isn't as dodgy as it looks from the outside, which is a relief. A few red-faced, beer-bellied regulars look up with interest as we make our way to the bar but we steam past them and into the saloon, which is completely empty. Angel keeps ordering us double whiskies, which I think are more for her benefit than mine.

Angel was born Angelo. She was an exceptionally pretty little boy, with an English mother and an Italian father. Her home town was up in Yorkshire. She was the middle child with an older and younger sister, and as the only son of the family, her fascination with frocks had not gone down that well with her parents, particularly her father. Even as a small child she never wanted to behave as befitted her gender. Strangers were constantly alarming her mother by telling her what pretty daughters she had. Angel would then be dragged off crying and screaming to the hairdresser to have the hair she tried so hard to grow lopped off. Her fairly impressive cleavage was achieved courtesy of hormone pills which she has been taking for years, but she has not gone all the way. At this, she points coyly downwards so I get the point. I gulp down this new information with large shots of strong spirits.

I return home swaying slightly from all the alcohol I consumed as her story unfolded. As well as the gender bombshell I have seen another side of Angel tonight. I am used to her being invincible and always 'in character', like some bad ass Betty Boop. Tonight she revealed a different Angel – and not just in the matter of genitalia. She seems anxious that I am not too alarmed by it all. Despite her jokes she keeps glancing nervously at me, trying to gauge my real reaction. I try to reassure her by showing a great deal of superficial calm, realising that, shocked as I am, I'll get over it. Somehow I have a strong suspicion that it won't be the last of Angel's surprises.

CHAPTER 5

The next morning we follow the hangover ritual that Angel kindly introduced me to the day after she moved in. I am feeling sick and beseiged with information that I was not sober enough to ingest the night before. I don't mind what gender she started out as, it just feels odd to have developed a friendship with such a misconception in place. At first, though I tried my best to hide it, I felt confused, tricked almost, but I keep telling myself that nothing has really changed.

Angel has decided that following her revelation she no longer needs to wear make-up to breakfast. Without her well-applied slap she is two shades paler and has dark circles under her eyes to rival mine. There is still the unmistakable essence of Angel, with her perfectly arched eyebrows, but the look is more androgyne than Ava.

I would like to ask more questions but am aware that I have no right to, that she doesn't need to explain any more than she has. I am pleased that I have finally seen her naked face though; it makes me less conscious of how I look in the morning. We are a little more formal and polite to each other for a few days after my 'discovery', but only very subtly, and we soon lapse into our previous tone of communication. Angel is still Angel, after all.

'Uma, when are you going to get out of those raggedy old shorts and come clubbing with me and find yourself a nice feller?'

'Judging by the lovely specimens I've seen you having breakfast with, I don't think so.'

'What do you mean? Simon was really good-looking and nicely put together.' 'Well-built' is a good description of Angel's male 'friends' as a lot of them do look a bit like human-sized Lego men in various different colours. In Angel's world it definitely is survival of the fittest rather than the brightest. I was surprised to see that the last shining example of manhood to emerge from her room could manage a knife and fork.

'You're too fussy, Uma. Okay, he didn't have that much up top, but looks and the ability to drive me about in a nice car are what really matter.'

Angel's origins do not seem to worry any of the men that appear occasionally after she's been out of an evening. They are a strange bunch – generally very butch (in the straight sense not in the Leather One from Village People sense), yet they are keen as mustard to come home with my beautiful friend. According to Angel it is purely due to her sensational looks and the fact that she makes a real effort when she goes out. I think there may be a lot more to it than that, but I can't fathom exactly what's going on in their minds, and I have my suspicions that most of them aren't too sure either.

As we continue our friendship I find it surprisingly easy to forget that there is a discrepancy between Angel's womanliness and her particular bits and pieces. I am starting to understand what she means by one of her favourite sayings: 'You are what you choose to be'. When she first said it I thought it was just a dig at me to wear more make-up.

CHAPTER 6

Good fortune finally sends me a commission for some illustration work. I clear my desk which has become a dumping ground for oddments and get on with some initial sketches. By a wonderful coincidence they are to accompany an article on cross-dressing for a women's magazine, though it is mostly about a very different type of cross-dresser – the sort that wives discover unexpectedly parading around in their best silk undies. I still find myself drawing Angel's huge blonde confection of a hairstyle on a siren's figure with enormous feet.

Angel sweeps down the stairs in a wonderful outfit of unprecedented glamour, stands for a while in the kitchen in a taa-daa style waiting for my compliments which I give wholeheartedly, and then the toot of a cab calls her away. It is no ordinary cab that whisks her off, but a big black Mercedes limousine. I can see the faces of the neighbours directly opposite peering out as Angel, relishing the scene, takes her time organising her things and finally gets in. As a not altogether uncurious person I am twitching with questions and she knows it. She throws me a gracious smile, raises her eyebrows to the heavens and leaves.

I work solidly for the next few hours, and just as I finish off the last drawing, I hear the car that Angel disappeared in arrive outside my house. She returns, drunk and slightly smudged, then hotfoots it upstairs and crashes out. I hear the purr of a gentle snore float out on to the landing and I am left without any explanation of her outing. Sulkily I turn on some music, cranking up the volume in an attempt to rouse her. I love the stories of her extravagant exploits.

She sleeps most of the evening, leaving me to finish off the bottle of red wine we abandoned the night before. I have enough sense to laugh at myself and my annoyance – I am the one who wanted a 'self-contained' lodger. I shouldn't be hovering around the landing with all the bitterness of a thwarted gossip.

I am feeling more than just curiosity, however. Something in Angel's flash outing has awakened a sense of adventure I didn't believe I still possessed. I am vaguely aware of a niggling feeling, an itch of dissatisfaction that is starting to want some action of my own.

Angel re-emerges later that night. She comes downstairs slightly sozzled and disorientated, unsure of what time of day it is. I am waiting for her with a big, conspiratorial, Cheshire cat grin on my face as she finally appears, her make up and hair having grown in her sleep, give her a

Heavy Metal appearance. Her answers are infuriatingly and uncharacteristically prim.

'So who were you meeting this afternoon?'

'A friend. Just an old friend.'

'A rich old friend? Hence the limousine.'

'I s'pose he is.'

Angel is never short of words to describe people. Generally she will come out with an extremely funny account of the person in question. This time I cannot bash through her reticence. Whatever angle I try I get nowhere. I have become accustomed to Angel being frank; too frank sometimes as she sledgehammers any wrong ideas she feels I have when it comes to interior design or personal fashion. I am not used to her being discreet. We watch the television in a stubborn silence before I drift off to bed leaving her concentrating on a documentary on harsh conditions in the Arctic.

Angel, I suppose, is having her own adventure. It has certainly distracted her from her work. She makes enormous mirrors for overpriced, fashionable shops in the City and Islington. To create her masterpieces she uses bandages or, for the last one, clothes she has persuaded me are no longer wearable. She completes the whole effect with a can of gold spray paint, pops on a three-figure price tag and hopes the whole thing won't unravel in the cab on the way there. She has made two in the three weeks she has lived with me. I have tried to encourage her to be more productive, but since she informed me that we can't live without cable she has taken to sitting in front of TV talk shows all day and calling me to the television every twenty minutes to watch some scary small-town Americans slug it out on air. I have started to suspect she has a sugar daddy hidden some place, her very own Daddy Warbucks, as inactivity doesn't seem to dent her finances.

She seems to have a lot more energy in the evenings. She is like a caged bear when it gets dark; almost every night she would like to go somewhere. So far I have been unwilling to accompany her. I fill with panic at the idea of the two of us going out on the town. There is a horrible inevitability about it all: we will drink far too much and probably get into some sort of trouble. From the tales I have heard, Angel attracts trouble like a static charge attracts dust, and until now I have been cautious. She usually goes out anyhow, flouncing out of the bathroom with a defiant air, downs a few convivial drinks with me and then departs in a cab, a fall-out of expensive perfume wafting behind her.

I am left at home, grateful for the safety of my sofa but not completely immune to Angel's adventurousness. It is slowly dawning on me that there is a limit to how safe one needs to be when under the age of thirty. I may have lost a not-so-perfect husband somewhere along the line but I seem to have found a perfect partner for adventure.

On the fourth Friday since she landed on my doorstep I decide that it would not hurt to live a little. Feeling flush with a whole month's rent that Angel has handed me, I announce, to her amazement, that I fancy a night out. She insists that she *must* do my make-up. We have quite different ideas about my face: I claim that I do apply make-up when I go out, and she swears that I am not wearing any. We compromise, with

Angel giving me what she calls her 'natural look'. The effect is kind of shocking when I first see myself in the mirror but I get used to it. I look like a tart, but an expertly made-up one. I have also been persuaded to wear my hair down, which I generally find nerve-racking, at least in hot places, as my curls tend to expand and leave me looking like Crystal Tipps on acid. Angel has other ideas. She has been torturing my hair for a good half an hour with a pair of hot tongs so I have Farrah Fawcett (before she lost it) waves. To keep this marvellous effect I am viciously sprayed with half a can of pungent spray. I can still taste it at the back of my throat and floating round my lungs when we finally get round to leaving the house. Even the three brandies we drink to get ourselves in the mood don't wash the taste away.

I do look good, I tell myself, emboldened by alcohol, as I do one last check before we are out the door. The final touch is a pair of heels. I need no bullying to wear these. Every five foot two and a half inches of me loves to wear high heel shoes. It is only due to the practicality of actually having to walk places that prevents me from swanning around all day shod like Carmen Miranda. If I could live my life with the assistance of a chauffeur then I would never wear remotely flat shoes ever again. However, as reality has meant having to dodge kerb crawlers as I walk back from Whitechapel tube station I have grown to neglect anything other than sensible footwear. It is great to find an excuse to be reacquainted with gloriously sexy shoes.

Angel is impressed when I emerge four inches taller; I don't think she's ever suspected the slut within me. I think she is also fairly pleased with the overall transformation for which she takes most of the credit. I leave in a perfect state for entering a club – slightly drunk and smug as hell.

Angel has called the shots on the location of our evening out. Her choice seems to be dictated by the fact that she has had intimate knowledge of the bouncer at this particular venue and so we will be able to avoid the unnecessary inconvenience of having to queue or pay. The place is in some warehouse that has been tarted up with a large amount of cheap red velvet and massive white screens suspended from the ceiling. Clips of what looks like cheesy 1970s porn films are bounced off the walls, an effect made even stranger by the fact that the dialogue is drowned out by the music from the dance floor. There is a really tiny transvestite, who I would conservatively estimate to be in her early sixties, doing a heart-rending version of 'Lola' on the stage at the far end. She has the face of a powdered raisin and bright orange lipstick but the most stunning floor-length silver, beaded dress. When I look round Angel is already being chatted up by a topless Italian man wearing a cute choker saying 'FUCK' and a metal chain suspended from both his nipples. He keeps leaning his sweaty chest against her arm so he can whisper in her ear.

I am definitely not on my sofa any more. An old man in nothing but a short pleated PVC version of a tennis skirt sticks his nose down my cleavage and asks if I'm a 'real girl'. I am lost for the right reply but nod at him and he wanders off disappointedly. I'm starting to feel a little out of place when Angel grabs me and drags me over to the bar. I can tell when her eyes start scanning over my shoulder, after we finally manage to get served, that she is on the pull. What she lacks in subtlety she makes up for in *cojones*. Angel is on a mission and is soon off, performing a really sleazy salsa-type dance with a tall Rastafarian in a dapper suit. I am whiplashed by stray dreads as the pair of them get more and more carried away with their dancing. I remind myself that I am looking uncharacteristically foxy and stand nonchalantly pouting into the distance. There is one drawback to being blind enough to be able to convince myself I look like a Charlie's Angel, however: the almost complete inability to make out anything or anyone more than two feet away. The place is really dark, which compounds my myopia even further. One moment I am stepping back to avoid a big knot of hair jauntily slapping into my face and the next the two of them have gone. I comfort myself with the fact that I've been stranded only a few feet from the bar so at least I won't have to walk around in circles forlornly in search of my next drink. I am perhaps a little too near the bar for my liking, though. I don't feel all that comfortable standing here on my own. I order two drinks in case Angel returns soon, and prop myself up in the quietest corner I can find.

I try to locate Angel on the main dance floor. Normally I can just about make out the silhouette of her hair floating nimbus-like above crowds, but she doesn't seem to be there. At my elbow is a plump skinhead in bright blue eyeshadow, wearing higher heels than myself but still about three inches shorter. He is trying to catch my attention in a flirtatious way but my height advantage helps me avoid hearing what he's trying to tell me. I give him my wide, glazed, 'I don't know what you're saying but thanks anyway' smile and he drifts away. I would like to dance; I haven't danced for a very long time.

I feel as limber as the tin man when I eventually make my way unsteadily to the dance floor, but what the hell; the only person I actually know there is probably fused together with her dreadlocked dancing partner in some dark corner. I loosen up quite quickly when I realise that my recent life of grumpy solitude has not removed my ability to enjoy dancing. I can now be among large groups of people intent on enjoying themselves without feeling like an imposter.

'Hello.' Somebody taller than me, immediately identifiable as male and within the same generation is attempting to make contact. I grin back blindly. Brandy and music are starting to warm me up. I like this place. I like looking like a Seventies hooker and dancing only with my hips and arms because my heels are too high for foot movement. Life is sweet.

'You look great.'

'Thank you,' I say, with puzzled gratitude at an unexpected compliment.

'Really convincing.'

'Hmm. Actually I'm a girl. I mean, I was born a girl.' Maybe Angel's idea of what constitutes a 'natural look' is a little off-balance.

'Even better. I'm really sorry, it just gets confusing in here sometimes.'

We're left in silence, which is not too bad because we never really stopped dancing, just kind of slowed down. I am trying to work out what I feel about a man who might have fancied me if I had a dick; and wondering whether he still does now he knows I don't. He is the most promising member of the opposite sex that I have talked to for a while. Not that there has been even a hint of an offer since I waved goodbye to my chance of participating on *Mr & Mrs*. I try and size up what he really looks like, taking poor lighting and my short sight into consideration. As far as I can tell he is not all that bad. Probably a few years younger than me and dressed in such a normal fashion – jeans and a black tee-shirt – that he looks slightly out of place. In this light at least I can't make out any distinctively odd features; he is definitely dark-haired (I have an uncontrollable fear of blond men's genitals, something I've traced back to a litter of albino mice in my childhood). What he really has in his favour is that he can dance well. I have never in my twenty-seven years ever got together with a man who can dance. It is something I feel I have missed out on. I'm sure Angel has probably got through a troupe of them.

Just when I start to feel totally unconcerned about the exact whereabouts of Angel she appears, with bigger hair and minus her lipstick.

'There you are. Let's go to the bathroom. I need to check my face,' she says with a smirk, which suggests she's been having fun elsewhere.

'I'm fine.'

'Sure you don't need to reapply anything?'

'I'm sure.'

'Some more powder?'

'No, I've got so much on it'll last me all week.'

Angel evidently wants me to go with her. I'm quite happy staying where I am. She eventually gives up and disappears for another hour or so, leaving me grinning at my dancing boy.

CHAPTER 7

Despite Angel's obvious success earlier tonight, I'm the one who is sitting in the cab with what I hope could be a conquest at my elbow. Angel is chain smoking in sulky silence. The cab driver insists that she open the window to let some of the smoke out, and blasts of cold air lift my solid Farrah-style wings up and down over my face in an irritating flapping motion. I am horribly conscious of how rock hard my hair is. Angel refuses to speak as she is still in a state of agitation due to the disappearance of the one she had chosen to take away. I am starting to feel too shy and sleepy to make much of an effort so we sit in cramped silence gazing out of the window.

Back home, Angel perks up when she remembers that we still have nearly half a bottle of brandy left. She pours a good measure of that into her glass, adds a dash of coke and settles down in the living room. I have lost my bravado now. The little fellow I have lured back to my place seems nice enough but I'm having difficulty in visualising him in my bed. I try and imagine what he will look like without clothes on.

When I look across at Angel she seems to be engaged in the same visualisation process. Here is my salvation – a combination of being too timid and too drunk to care has hit in. I guiltily excuse myself and slip off to bed alone, giving Angel a friendly wink as I leave.

I am not completely convinced by this plan. I hover at the top of the stairs for a while trying to decide whether to swoop back like a harpy into the living room and airlift him straight up to my bedroom. Then I catch sight of my blurred reflection in the mirror and decide to leave any seduction to Angel.

When I finally rouse myself the following day I am a lot less happy with my decision. I have a filthy hangover and I haven't even had the filthy night to accompany it. Angel never seems to be as badly afflicted as I am with the aftermath of a night of heavy drinking; she will probably feel great this morning. I come downstairs to find her already up, with a huge smile on her face. I am deeply suspicious of this smile. It is peevish of me, I know, as I was the one who abandoned my prey to her but I am not feeling so generous this morning. Frustrated at my own cowardice is a more accurate description of my mood. I cannot tell whether our visitor has left or not, and I keep expecting him to pop up somewhere in the kitchen.

'He's gone,' she says, smirking at me.

'Nice night?'

'Very nice night.'

'Did you two get up to anything?'

'Not *really*.'

I don't want to hear what happened but I have to know. And I can tell by her face that she is more than willing to spill the beans.

'So how much is not really? You can tell me – I did find our little friend in the first place.'

'Well, actually nothing. I think he's more into your sort of girl – without any extras. He was nice though. We stayed up and talked for a bit, then he got a cab home. I don't know why you dumped him in the living room. Lovely green eyes *and* he owns a Ducati – that's a big motorbike to you, Uma. He works in Spitalfields, making websites for big companies or something like that. Not a bad catch if you'd bothered to reel him in.'

Thanks to Angel's information the morning suddenly seems a lot brighter. Lack of success is something best shared with those closest to you. I try to conceal my jubilation but fail miserably.

'I don't know why you look so pleased. You left him and buggered off to bed.'

'I'm just out of practice, that's all. It's been a long time.'

'Well you're never going to be *in* practice if that's the way you play it.'

'Let's just wait and see, shall we?'

On my bedroom floor, buried beneath the clothes I wore last night, is a phone number which may well be resurrected.

I have, somewhere deep in my befuddled scheme of things, a plan, but it will have to be put on ice for now. Today has been designated a day of shopping. Angel and I need to revive our dusty disco wings and get ourselves some new things to wear. I'm the one who really needs the overhaul but Angel is never one to opt out of a shopping expedition.

We haven't quite got the stomach for the West End on a Saturday so we decide to put our fashion flair to the test in Whitechapel Market and Brick Lane. We are very fortunate to live within walking distance of these two shopping Meccas. Walking to places is a new ability that I am trying to teach Angel. Her cash flow tends to be a little erratic so it's a skill that I'm trying to convince her could come in handy one day.

Whitechapel Market is the place, rivalled only by Roman Road, for incredible high street fashion bargains (most with their labels cut out), very cheap, brightly coloured saris and smart Indian suits. These are sold alongside boxes of gold sandals, mop heads and mangoes, and everything has a suspiciously low price. Angel loves shopping here; she only likes things to look expensive – she doesn't actually like to part with large sums of money if she can help it. Brick Lane is the source of an enormous selection of beautiful fabric: fake fur, tasselled trimmings, metres of maribou – all those essentials for a great outfit.

It's strange that I've become the one to persuade Angel to overcome her dislike for daytime crowds so she can hunt for bargains. I have even managed to get her to stroll with me to lunch at a few of the nicer local cafés. And just once

I got her to go to the cinema that has recently opened not far from where we live. She said she enjoyed it but I could tell that she found it really difficult to keep her mouth shut for the whole length of the film. Angel is not used to being an audience.

Any daytime outing that we do go on tends to involve me constantly assuring her that everyone isn't looking at her because they're questioning her gender. Generally, the looks she gets have more to do with the fact that she's a lot more glam than your average Stepney housewife.

Shopping with Angel is always an experience, and not an altogether unhazardous one. Sometimes I think it's a shame she's not blessed with poorer sight.

'What the hell is he looking at?' Angel snarls at one passer-by and attempts to follow him into a shop to give him a piece of her mind.

'Angel, we're in the East End. You are six feet tall, in full make-up and look like you've just stepped off the pages of *Vogue*. Of course he's looking at you.'

'Rude bastard. I'm going over there to tell him what a rude bastard he is. Looking at *me* like I'm a freak – with a haircut like his!'

'Let's just shop . . . please.'

Sometimes I feel like I'm walking round with a transsexual pit bull. What she lacks in calm she does make up for in style, though. We buy some great fabric – diaphanous pale violet stuff with a green design around the edge, ten metres of cheap silver lamé, a load of those tiny little tops which are made to be worn modestly under a sari and look fabulous worn tight and on their own over a generous, immodest chest, a large amount of gold effect jewellery, and to top it all off, a floor-length suede coat. The last purchase is my great extravagance but Angel manages to chat up the sales assistant so I get a healthy reduction. She just has to promise to go out to dinner with him in the future. I think we'll avoid that shop for a while as he isn't exactly dream date material.

I have now purchased all the necessary ingredients for my transformation. Never mind the kitchen, I am the one that is badly in need of redecoration. I have managed to dig out an old sewing machine that was lent to me by my mother about ten years ago, and as neither she nor I actually ever used the thing it has remained with me, disgarded and forgotten. I wipe off the thick layer of dust before I place my precious fabric underneath the needle. Angel is going to teach me how to sew; how to create the essential outfits to take me from house mouse to hot chick.

I am as excited as a keen five year old on their first day of school as I wait for Angel. She has gone upstairs to answer a call on her mobile phone. I find this habit of hers puzzling. She is not a shy person; I generally know more than I want to about her personal habits. So why can't I listen in on her phone calls? Considering that she is not all that energetic when not rocket-fueled by alcohol, it always amazes me to see her thundering up and down the stairs every time her phone rings. Tonight I can hear the tone of her voice, hard and petulant, and I am left to sit at the machine, my hands clutching at the ends of my fabric, and wonder who it is.

'Uma.' My name floats down the stairs waveringly. It sounds as though a request is to be made.

'Mmm, what do you want?'

'Well . . . a friend of mine wants to pop by just for a short while. A male friend, is that okay?'

'Of course it is! You don't normally ask my permission. I haven't introduced a household rule that stops you seeing men just because I haven't got lucky for a while.'

'Great. He'll be here soon. I'll entertain him in my room.'

When he eventually arrives I am about to sew two bits of roughly my size pieces of fabric together. Angel moves superfast towards the door. Her speed is not explained in the brief glimpse I have of her visitor before she expresses him up the stairs. He is not what I have grown to think of as Angel's 'type', even though this encompasses quite a large number of different males. He is a good five inches shorter than her, mid-forties with a Jack Nicholson hairline. I can't help thinking that something strange is going on in my spare room.

If I thought he was genuinely a dear old friend I probably would not be averse to keeping an eye (well, an ear at least) on the proceedings. However, I have a strong feeling that I really don't want to be spying on this little interaction.

Less than half an hour later he's gone, whizzing out of the front door without even a backward glance.

This time it is my voice that rises unsteadily up the stairs.

'Angel – I think we need a little talk.' There is a silence

and I sense she does not want to come down. I can hear her shifting in her room but she doesn't emerge. I wait patiently. I have forgotten all about my sewing lesson. It has been superceded by what I suspect might be the second of Angel's revelations.

She eventually trundles down the stairs. This time I am determined not to be quite as blunt as I was in the matter of her gender. I don't think that she particularly wants to talk to me right now, but my fears that my house is going to turn into a sleazy bordello are too strong to put off this chat for another day.

'Angel, did you know that man before he turned up tonight?'

'Sort of . . . 'course I did.'

'What's his name? How do you know him?'

'John, met him in a bar,' she says breezily. Then she looks at me and smirks. I sit opposite her with a hard look on my face.

'Okay then,' she finally cracks. 'I don't know him. He's a client. I have to earn a living, don't I?'

I nod slowly. I am not even that surprised; it would take an awful lot of overpriced mirrors to finance Angel's lifestyle. I had suspected something a little more glamorous though. I feel uncomfortable questioning her in such a prissy manner. It is her room. On the other hand I'm not too keen on the idea of a mixed bag of sexually frustrated men wandering about my landing; not ones I haven't chosen, anyway.

'What happens if your clients turn out to be nutters?'

'I can look after myself.' At six feet and thirteen stone

she's probably right, but I am rediscovering my conventional side. I am only vaguely ill at ease at what Angel does – if anyone can handle such a profession it's her. What has alarmed me is the *in my house* syndrome. I do try and cling to the right side of the law, more or less, give or take a spot of tax evasion, and my paranoia is now projecting pictures into my mind of me standing in a Victorian courtroom being sentenced to ten years' hard labour for running a bawdy house. I am too neurotic to break the law.

To ease the atmosphere I change the subject for the moment, much to Angel's relief, and we get back to the rudiments of my sewing lesson.

CHAPTER 8

A few more strangers have been fast tracked up the stairs since then. We have agreed that her visitors can drop by only when I'm elsewhere, my thinking being that if I'm not actually about when she conducts her business it will be less of a reality. There has been a strange silence between us over the matter. Angel has made a few quips now and then, but I have said very little. This does not mean it hasn't been rattling around my head. I am just lost for a solution at present.

I have made great progress with my sewing machine. My masterpiece is the transformation of the silver lamé into a full-length, fishtail skirt, which hides a pair of enormous heels sprayed silver by Angel. I look like some mythical creature, a metallic mermaid from the future. I love it. It is not something I could wear on a great number of occasions but we have managed to come up with a suitable venue for its first outing. We have decided upon a ball. Not a society ball with chinless inbreds in dinner jackets throwing bread rolls at each other, but a drag ball, with double glazing salesmen from Dagenham resplendent in sequins for the night. I'm really excited. A ball's a ball and I need somewhere that I can shine. I'm feeling particularly buoyant. I can't stop singing verses from the 'Ugly Bug Ball'. The song has got hold of my head and when I'm not actually singing it, I'm humming the tune.

'Will you stop that!'

'What?'

'Singing that bloody song.'

'I can't – I'm in a really good mood.'

'Where's this come from? What are you up to?'

'Nothing. I've just got an amazing outfit, a glamorous friend to accompany me, and a hot date.'

'Who? You haven't been out the house since we went out together that Friday . . . Is that who you're meeting? Crafty cow! When did you get hold of him?'

'This morning. I dug out his number and when you were out and about with one of your 'patients', I invited him to meet us there.'

'It's about time you got up to something. You live like a nun.'

'Not tonight, my dear Angel, not tonight!'

Nuns don't wear silver lamé, except perhaps killer nuns, and they tend to be Spanish. Angel is going to torture my hair into submission again and slap on the make-up so I am virtually unrecognisable from my everyday self. Sod natural – tonight overblown is definitely called for. Angel has gone for a very understated semi-transparent black lace number. We had a full rehearsal and her dress requires a corset laced so tightly I nearly skinned my knuckles trying to wrench it together. I have no idea how she will be able to sit down in the cab; I am concerned that we may have to request one with a sunroof. I have the opposite problem in that I have made my skirt a little too large and have to tuck the waistband into my pants to keep the whole thing up. Anyway, despite our underpinnings, we look pretty damn good on the outside. Angel is right – it is all about artifice and attitude.

Somehow we manage to get Angel into an executive mini-cab. She has to lie across the back seat so I sit in the front. Our 'executive' car doesn't seem all that different from a normal cab except that we have been given a much better-looking driver than normal. Angel notices this before we even climb in and is now trying to make a move on him from her recumbent position in the back. He looks very nervous but we manage to get him to agree to return pumpkin-like at the end of the night and carry us back home.

We both exit the cab with some difficulty, like a pair of drunken mummies rising out of a sarcophagus. Glamour isn't easy. The place we go to is an East End hall that has been decked out to look like something out of a 1950s musical, with wall-to-wall glitter curtains and multi-coloured fairy lights. All around us are men with varying degrees of ability to pass for women; some are young, beautiful and completely convincing, others looking like dockers in drag.

55

No one has held back on the fantasy stakes: there are wigs as big as window frames, dresses with huge hooped skirts, and a whole range of outrageous outfits that would make a Hollywood starlet look drab.

The wonderful thing about these clubs is the space allowance people make for one another's costumes. My fishtail is given real respect. I suppose it's because clothes maketh the transvestite, after all. Angel is physically unable to sit down so we have to stand at the bar.

'There you are! I've been waiting for you.' I look up and think it must be a case of mistaken identity as I'm being addressed by a tall trannie with a black bob and big red lips. I do what I always do in these situations and grin gormlessly until I work out who I'm talking to.

'You don't recognise me! It's Matt. Well, actually it's Marla tonight.'

'Oh my God, it's you! I'm sorry, I just didn't expect you to be all dressed up . . . Wow! You look great . . . you really do. I didn't realise you were into all this stuff.'

'I'm kind of a novice.'

'Me too. I haven't dressed like a mermaid ever before.'

Angel has caught on now and her eyebrows are smirking at me over the top of her wine glass. Bitch! She knows I'm suffering. I wasn't expecting to have to compete with my date for the 'Belle of the Ball' title. This is not quite how I expected my first non-marital liaison to kick off. Despite the fact that I'm smiling amiably at him I am a little taken aback. What the hell is this going to translate to in the bedroom? Still, at least I haven't been stood up.

He looks good, though. Very different from what I had envisaged, but thankfully he does it quite well. I may have bolted if he'd turned up in something nastily frumpy. I toss him a few compliments to cover up the fact that I was initially a bit thrown. He probably didn't expect me to turn up looking like I'd just fallen off the front of a ship. Now I'm even more confused about our potential pairing, but awash with brandy I'm not really thinking about anything too deeply.

The outfits Angel and I constructed are going down a storm. We're having a great pose standing in the hallway fielding compliments from passers-by. I nearly lose my trannie date behind the big feathered skirts of an admiring possé of drag queens with beehives. I grab his hand so he's not swept off with the crowd. I'm not quite sure what I make of all this but I'd like to leave my options open. My love life has been lacking for too long to make any rash decisions based on the fact that the fellow in question is wearing too much lipstick and has too little leg hair. As a child I was never very keen on playing with dollies, but now I'm a grown-up I might make an exception for a man-sized one.

It is truly a ball. Angel and I finally make our way on to the dance floor after holding court at the bar for a while. Drunk and dressed inappropriately for actual movement, we shimmy beautifully for a few hours. When we are too tired to show off any longer I lurch, lips puckered, at my date for the evening. I've ceased to worry about what he is wearing. My earlier concerns have been replaced by a certain horniness and now I don't think I would care if he was wearing a teapot. I simply want to know whether there is a chance that, later on, neither of us will be wearing anything at all.

I'd never realised what a hazard it can be kissing someone who is also wearing make-up. I don't know how lipstick lesbians manage. Angel kindly lends me her compact so I can mop up the red oil slick left around my mouth. Apart from the Ronald McDonald after effect, it is perfectly fine.

After a great deal of posing and shimmying we leave, the three of us together, a drunken blur of shiny fabric, big hair and lip gloss.

CHAPTER 9

My deep sleep is broken by the persistent ringing of the telephone. The first thing I see is a wig on my bedroom floor, a flesh-coloured silicone breast peeping out from underneath it. Next to me in my bed is a sleeping man, his face smudged black and red with yesterday's make-up. There is something comforting about this. The wonderful thing about getting drunk and falling straight into bed with a trannie is that the next morning *both* of you will wake up looking like members of Kiss. I stagger down to the phone in a state of confusion. I think it must be really early in the morning and that the insistent ringing of the phone must mean some calamity.

Angel evidently never made it upstairs to go to sleep. She has collapsed on the sofa half out of her dress, her corset still on but unlaced so it looks like it's exploded in the night. She's snoring deeply, her head buried under one of the cushions.

I pick up the phone.

'Hello, Uma.' An extremely familiar voice reminds me that I still have a husband somewhere.

'It's you. What are you doing ringing so early?'

'It's two thirty in the afternoon. What's wrong with you? You sound awful.'

'I've just woken up,' I croak back at him. 'Look, this is a really bad time. Please just let me go back to bed and ring me again some time in the week and we'll have a chat.' I'm too hungover to be able to give him an appropriate response.

'*Have a chat*! I am still married to you and we haven't spoken for nearly three months. Don't you think it's important for us to sit down and work out what the hell is going on? I want to come over and see you.'

'Now? That's really not a good idea.'

'Why not?'

I take a deep breath and think about the real reason: because there is a man in my bed wearing my nightie and a semi-naked transsexual comatose on the sofa.

'It's just very bad timing, that's all. Try me again on a day that isn't today.' I put the phone down sharply and hope I've deterred him sufficiently to keep him from turning up on my doorstep.

Before I go back to bed I mop up some of the make-up overflow around my eyes. I look almost human by the time I gently ease myself under the covers.

I snuggle down, but I'm too aware of the fact that there is a stranger less than a foot away to be able to go back to sleep. I am also in that uncomfortable limbo land that

60

excessive alcohol sometimes leaves me in; I hurt too much to sleep, but it is too painful to actually get out of bed, so I am left in this strange state of suspended animation where I just lie very still and try not to register the assorted waves of pain coming from my head and stomach.

I'm brought back to the land of the living by a hand on my thigh. It sits there awkwardly for a while. I've been put off my stride, haunted by the image of my husband standing in a local phone box or, worse still, steaming down my street with a set of keys in his hand. Funnily enough, I can't seem to remember him all that clearly; it's strange how you can fail to look at people you're too familiar with. All I can see in my mind is that stroppy, tight little mouth of his as he resolutely stomped out of the house on that final Sunday. It is not a particularly pleasant image. He could burst through the front door at any moment. To turn up unwanted wouldn't really be in his nature, but as mine is verging on the neurotic I lie in bed with a strange leaden hand on my leg, jangling my nerves.

Eventually, due to the lack of any reaction from me, the hand is removed. I feel a slight twinge of guilt as I remember that the night before I had been very responsive. That was until I drunkenly passed out before we got very far along the road of sexual discovery. Confusing him is as valid a technique as any other in the art of seduction, I suppose. We lie in silence for a while. I'm still pretending to be half asleep until my brain is sufficiently in gear to deal with the situation.

He leans over my pretend asleep face. 'Good morning,'

61

he says hesitantly. I flutter my eyelashes in a graceful, just waking up fashion. It's a good thing he hadn't woken up earlier or I wouldn't have been able to prise my eyelids apart immediately due to the build up of last night's eyelash glue. As it is, at least I look like the kind of girl that doesn't soil pillows – unlike my companion who's looking severely Rocky Horror this morning. I do my angel of mercy bit and fetch him something to clean his face and some cotton buds. This will give me the added bonus of seeing him in daylight, without make-up and relatively sober. I don't want to have breakfast with the guy and then discover that he's pig ugly.

His face, once clean, is a really pleasant surprise. I wasn't intending to judge him that harshly as I'm sure I don't look too peachy this morning, but I find on close inspection I've actually done very well for myself. I'm not too sure what I make of his cross-dressing tendencies but he does look rather lovely with nothing on. All of a sudden those images of a husband marching up the stairs are beginning to fade away, and I'm not in so much of a hurry to leap straight out of bed.

Someone raps on the front door briskly and I sit up like a frightened rabbit caught in the wrong warren. I'm not used to bedroom farce situations. For three months I haven't even been in a bedroom situation. I am frozen to the spot, sitting upright in bed, the covers pulled up to my chin, though it isn't me I have to hide. I start desperately searching around in my pained block of a head for the name of the naked man who is sitting on the edge of my bed. Matt! I remember triumphantly. I can now answer if anyone demands: who is this man? I can hear Angel roll off the sofa and make a clumsy path to the door. I want to stop her but I know that if it is my husband he has keys anyway, and I don't want to make myself seem any more dodgy to the man at the end of my bed. He may think I'm a bit too strange if I scream down the stairs: 'Don't open the door!' It might be Angel's Avon lady after all.

It is not Angel's Avon lady. It's not even the dreaded husband. It's my mother. I decide that I must have incurred some ancient curse that's in place purely to scupper my sex life. Just for once I have a sort of adulterous and as yet unconsummated attempt at a one-night stand and fate throws my mother into the proceedings. From the sounds coming from downstairs I can tell that Angel is taking her through to the kitchen. I am not good in difficult situations; I have an unfortunate tendency to become rather witless when surprised. Luckily, Angel is much better at thinking on her feet. She is also a superb liar. She knocks gently on my bedroom door. Her face is wearing one enormous, cheeky grin.

'Uma, dear, your mother's downstairs.'

I open the door a fraction and eye her suspiciously through the crack. She has the sofa throw wrapped around herself like some Indian squaw. God knows what my mother is thinking. Angel glances at the other occupant of the room who has covered himself up with lightning speed. 'You can put your friend in my room until the coast is clear,' she whispers.

'I'll . . . just keep out of the way,' he says, looking almost as mortified as I do as he's led off to Angel's bedroom wearing only a small towel. I realise that the only clothes he has are what he was wearing last night. Just another little conundrum to add to everything else.

I decide that I can't worry too much about him right now. I'll let Angel hide him for the time being, deal with my mother, and then sort him out. I'm aware that this is not the smoothest start to an affair but I'll have to deal with the full implication and embarrassment of that later. For now I have to get myself down the stairs. I manage to put on a dress, the variety that you can pull over your head – I'm not together enough to deal with zips or buttons – and make my way shakily to the living room.

My mother has already started tidying up the collection of empty bottles and glasses that litter my kitchen surfaces. At the best of times she looks nothing like me; right now we appear to be from different species. She is taller and less voluptuous, with hair that on anyone else I would call dishwater blonde, but as it's my mother I describe it as dark blonde. It is also totally kink free, lopped in a sensible bob. Her diametrically opposed attributes to my own enable her to look smart and reliable at all times. She could survive a shipwreck and look unruffled, whereas I always look as if I've just crawled out of a catastrophe. She not only looks together but is in possession of unnaturally large quantities of calm.

'Late night was it?' She smiles indulgently at me, fixing me with her large, grey-blue, ever-trusting eyes. I give her a sickly grin. 'Sorry to just drop in on you like this but you've been impossible to reach on the phone. Quite a few people called me to try and find out where you were so I got a little worried. I was coming to London anyway to visit a friend, and it seemed such a waste not to come and check on my only daughter.'

'I'm fine. Still getting bits and pieces of work. Everything's great.'

'The girl who opened the door seems nice, very friendly. Did she go out with you last night?'

'Yes . . . she's staying here for a while. Paul and I are kind of taking time out from each other so Angel's living here instead. She rents the spare room.'

'When did all this happen?'

'A few months ago.'

'You never mentioned anything was wrong. It seems a strange way to work out any problems, if you don't mind me saying so.'

'It was his great idea. He rang this morning out of the blue, but I'm enjoying his absence a bit too much so you might have lost a son-in-law, I'm afraid.'

'I'm not all that bothered about having a son-in-law, but I am interested in my daughter. You should have let me know what was happening. I hate to think of you going through something so upsetting.'

'I managed. I just couldn't face ringing you to say that I'd messed everything up.'

'You didn't. If there's anyone to blame I'm sure it's Paul. Are you sure you're okay? You do look a little pasty.'

'That has nothing to do with my marriage, believe

me. I just have a bit of a headache from going out last night.'

My mother is looking at me with that kind yet inquisitive look of hers. I can hear the sound of two pairs of feet making their way down the stairs. Angel just cannot resist making an entrance. Behind her is Matt, for whom she has found some of her more unisex items of clothing. He is about four inches shorter than her and a good two stone lighter, but he looks what could pass for ordinary to my mother, who has never been all that observant of these things anyway. He glances at me sorrowfully as the two of them sweep into the room, his face trying to convey the fact that it wasn't his idea, but I'm already aware who was the leading force behind this.

Angel and my mum get on really well. They start an animated discussion of the shortcomings of the man to whom I had been married (despite the fact that Angel has never met him) and do most of the rest of the talking while I sit on the end of the table and look dazed. Together the two of them decide that my erstwhile partner didn't deserve me. I would be flattered if Angel wasn't making everything up, and if my desertion wasn't being discussed in front of someone I'd prefer *not* to think of me as a sad sap just yet. Matt sits there helplessly and is forced to listen to the pair of them dissect my marriage. Two hours later, my mother leaves after I promise to call her for a long chat soon.

'Lovely girl, that Angel,' she whispers in the hall. If only she knew. I close the door and remember that I still have to salvage something from the wreckage that has been made of last night's coup.

CHAPTER 10

He didn't run away. Though this may well have had more to do with the fact that it was broad daylight in the heart of the East End – and all that he had to exit in was a cocktail dress and a pair of black stilettos. Nevertheless, he stayed a while after my mother left which gave me a chance to try and communicate the fact that I wasn't a totally tragic case. I also managed to persuade Angel to stop tormenting him and agree to let him wear the rag bag of unisex clothing she had found him. The poor man left barefoot in a very odd ensemble with last night's drag in a carrier bag.

He has been in contact since, which under the circumstances is pretty good. We have made a tentative arrangement to meet. Sneakily, through various forms of espionage, I have worked out when Angel has her next big meeting with her mystery client, the one that sends the limousine. This should keep her out of the way and enable me to get up to some mischief of my own for once.

First I have to meet up with the prodigal husband. After our last phone call he has grown worried about the state of my mental health and keeps demanding a visit. I manage to dissuade him from actually coming to the house and we choose a dismally fashionable café bar in Islington in which to discuss the details of our détente.

Angel and I quarrel over the suitability of the clothes I have picked for this particular outing. She is horrified by my original choice.

'You can't go and meet your ex-husband looking like that.'

'I look okay. I don't look like I've made an effort for him.'

'Yes, but there's no need to look like a scrag.'

'I look relaxed, *not* scraggy.'

But I still end up changing three times until we reach a compromise and Angel stops looking at me incredulously. In the end I settle for something that I'm not particularly comfortable in, but that doesn't look too dressed up and doesn't cause Angel's eyebrows to raise too high. I'm over half an hour late, but I reckon it's an abandoned wife's prerogative.

The place we have chosen is about as ill-disposed for this type of meeting as it is possible to be. It is fashionably sparse, with little metal tables positioned too close together and horrible, tiny chairs that make the backs of your legs sweat. It would be fine if we merely wanted to pose around and eavesdrop on other people's conversations. For discussing the nitty gritty of a defunct marriage we are painfully exposed. Apart from the two of us, there is a vacant-looking couple who are sitting far too close to our table and barely saying anything to each other. They're so quiet I'm convinced that they are tuned in to our conversation.

My former spouse is pale and unshaven. It's strange to face him after all this time. He looks different; it is as if I am looking at him through cack-coloured glasses. I notice the unpleasant hue of his suit and the slight bouffant nature of his hair and feel a wave of queasiness and hostility when I sit down next to him.

'You made it,' he says tersely, waving a menu at me.

'After such a long break I thought you could manage an extra half an hour,' I reply almost as sourly.

'Uma, we are here to sort things out.'

'Are we? What sort of things?'

'Us. The resuscitation of our marriage.'

'Three months is quite a long time to wait to bring something back to life. I think it might have started to decompose by now.'

'Don't say that. I'm sorry, what I did must have been really hurtful, but I'll never be put in that situation again.'

'What, living with me? Yes, that does seem highly unlikely right now.'

'No, I mean being unfaithful. Moving in with Nickie.'

'*What*! Who the hell is Nickie?'

'That's the name of the girl I've been living with.'

'You moved out to live with someone called *Nickie?*' I give a quick glance at the other table. If they are being nosy I bet they're having a field day right now. They're still both looking totally blank, but that could just be a cover-up. A waitress, one of those good-looking automatons they employ in these places, has made her slow, petulant way to our table and is waiting in silence, pen poised, to take our order. We break off and study the menu, I feel I'm going to need sustenance for the forthcoming fight. After ordering and watching her flat rump sashay back to the kitchen I am ready for the kill. I wasn't going to savage my cheating bastard husband under the nose of some snooty waitress.

'Let me get this right. You left me to go and live with someone you were already sleeping with?'

'Uma, that's all in the past. We're here to talk about our future together.' He tries to reach out and take hold of my hand but I'm really not in the mood for physical affection right now.

'Hang on a moment. I'm just catching up with what has actually been going on.'

'You knew this. You must have known . . . that's why you didn't try and phone me or anything.'

'I didn't call you because you left. What did you expect me to do – track you down and beg you to come home?'

'At the very least try and contact me.'

'Bearing in mind what you were up to it's a bloody good job I didn't bother, isn't it?'

'Uma, I thought you already knew all this.' His face is a perfect picture now he's realised he's given himself away. I am really going to make the most of this.

'So who or what is Nickie and where did she emerge from?'

'She works with me.'

'But the only people you work with are old men.' Taking into account what has been going on in my life lately a strange image briefly flickers into my head.

'She started quite recently.' I'm disappointed at this; I would have been much happier if it had been some old codger in a tiara.

'When did she start?'

'May.'

'You never mentioned anyone new popping up in your office. Probably because you had the idea in your sneaky little head all the time.'

The club-sandwich-bearing clone returns with my beer and a measly-looking sandwich buried under a handful of ornamental frilly lettuce. I gulp down half of it in one bite before embarking on my second onslaught.

'So you liked her enough to move in with her and shag her, but now you want to come back?'

'I was temporarily attracted to her. I have to apologise for that.'

'Oh, fuck off! You were supposed to be permanently attracted to me, you slimy bastard.'

'I've said I'm sorry. It was a big mistake, I fully realise that now. I deserve some credit for telling you the truth.'

'Yeah, by accident. It's more like you've slipped up in your own mess than actually come clean of your own accord.'

'It's completely finished now.'

'So what? Now I don't give a toss if you're sleeping with your entire office.'

In the beginning I was so stunned by his admission that I felt I was only play-acting angry, but I knew that the real stuff would kick in very quickly after the surprise element wore off. Now I can feel myself slowly rising to the gnashing-of-teeth level of furious. I am stupified that he can entertain the idea that there is even the remotest chance of a rerun. My bile ducts are on overdrive and I just sit and fume for a moment.

'Uma, I don't expect you to take me back just like that. Think it all over and I'll call you at the end of the week.'

'Like everything is going to radically change in a few days.'

'I know you – you'll think about things objectively and then you'll calm down.'

'I will not! Anyway, you can't come back, someone else has moved in.'

'A man?'

'Don't sound so shocked. Yes, a man. Obviously you don't know me quite as well as you think you do.' If we're talking chromosomes I am telling the truth, and I know Angel will forgive me for describing her as such if I explain exactly why.

'You didn't waste much time.'

'Excuse me. You didn't waste any time. There was in fact an overlap involved in your little peccadillo.'

'So you and this man . . .'

72

'Angelo.' Great, now he thinks I've got an Italian stallion to fill the stable.

'You moved him in when?'

'A few weeks after you left, and he's not moving. We're very happy living together.' I'm starting to enjoy this interchange a little more. The element of surprise is now slightly more evenly balanced between the two of us.

'So that's that? I can't believe you shacked up with someone just like that.' His idiotic tone of aggrieved pride would be funny if I wasn't so angry.

'You leg it with some slut from your office and you're upset?'

'I just didn't think it of you.'

'Surprises all round then.'

I have had enough. I've finished my designer sandwich, I've even sucked on that foul purple lettuce stuff that tastes like creosote. I leave him to pay the bill and do my best to make a good exit. One thing that living with Angel has taught me is the importance of a well-executed departure.

CHAPTER 11

In many ways I am lucky to have Angel as a housemate. Best of all is the fact that she has dated more pond life than perhaps any other living person. She can come up with a thousand and one ways to run down a lover. She also has a whole host of gasp-inspiring horror stories of her own; stories that make my desertion seem positively dreary. There was the boyfriend who got married to someone else and failed to mention it to her during their two-year relationship – he'd even explained away his wedding ring as a gift from his mother; another one that slept with her best friend (at the time) and relieved both of them of substantial amounts of cash and jewellery before disappearing rather suddenly. The list goes on and on, and is generally followed by Angel's complicated and vicious revenge schemes.

Perhaps what annoys me most about what has happened is the commonplace shabbiness of my husband's actions. As he had failed to mention the real reason why he was leaving, I had in my laughably short-sighted way not really considered that particular option. Someone from his office – it's such an unimaginative ending. Then again, imagination has never been his strong point.

Under the expert tutelage of Angel I am learning to relish and enhance every single aspect of his personality that ever annoyed me: from the way he could spend twenty minutes combing his thin, brown hair into a style he was deluded into thinking was sexy, to the inordinate amount of time he would spend scrubbing vegetables, not knowing that for years he had been eating every pesticide under the sun when I did the cooking in my straight-from-the-bag fashion. It is the small things that filled me with the most hate. I was with a man who for the last year of our marriage spoke to me as if he were indulging a loon, but what raises the most nausea is the fact that I stayed with someone who was proud of the fact that he sold advertising space for a living. This is what leaves me truly horrified.

Angel has taken to her role as my brand new boyfriend very well. She has taken to answering the phone with a low, masculine voice and an Italian accent. I am amazed at how well she can do this until she points out that this is the way nature intended her to sound. So far it has only managed to confuse my mother, but I'm sure it will prove useful at some point. I haven't heard anything more from the man who once lived here but I have a feeling that he will be buzzing around for a while. He always used to be such an obstinate little soul. I dreamt last night of his face on a tiny wasp body crawling about the plates as I was trying to enjoy a picnic.

There is a part of me that is pleased at the fact that now I don't have to make any tricky decisions. I am far too pissed off and stubborn ever to be able to stomach a reconciliation. On top of that I have absolutely no desire for him any more. And there is the added benefit that his actions have given a green light to my own affair, which wasn't quite off the starting blocks just yet. There will be a small yet delicious feeling of retribution if I do get lucky tonight.

I have taken every care that things will run smoothly. Angel will be whisked off in her limousine at eight o'clock. She's always very punctual for this arrangement, leaving me an hour and a half to prepare myself into a goddess and to dispose of any minor interruptions. Then, with the help of a lot of alcohol, we should be safely in bed well before Angel arrives home. I will be happy to fill her in on the details the next morning, just as she has kindly shared with me all her trysts (romantic, not financial ones) of the past weeks.

Angel's preparation started extra early this time. Her natural hair is in tiny plaits all over her head and the wonderfully voluminous blonde waves come in long strips which are sewn onto her own hair. I'm having to hack out some of the oldest chunks and replace them with new, white blonde streaks. This is not my favourite task. The new hair to go in is fragant and soft, the old stuff is resemblant of an old coconut mat that's been on the floor of one too many nightclubs. It also involves careful surgery with a tiny pair of scissors, in the innermost part of the weave. One false snip and our friendship could be severed.

Luckily there are no mishaps and she has a clean, shiny

head of brand new streaks by the time it comes to getting ready. I can hear her singing joyfully in the bath. Angel always comes back from these assignments with great wads of cash and that's truly the way to her heart. She is radiant by the time she is ready to leave and we hear the hoot of a big car pulling up beside the house. We drain our glasses of the champagne we bought, in celebration of all the bottles she will be able to buy after she receives her readies tonight.

From the window I watch her step into the car as elegantly as Cinderella (if Cinderella had been a modern day trannie call-girl). She throws me a wave and a kiss. Then I'm straight in the bathroom clutching the one essential ingredient to any romantic interlude – a razor. With Angel out of the way I'm free to light the candles – we both insist on candlelit bathing; high wattage can be too cruel when you're naked – fill the bath with bubbles and commandeer what's left of the champagne.

I feel good. I'm soft, fragrant and dimly lit – what more could a girl ask for? Apart from my date to turn up, perhaps, but I have a good feeling about this one. After all, I persuaded Angel to lend him some of her clothes to go home in. She was, purely for her own amusement, going to make him wear his little black dress so he owes me one.

Matt arrives a short while before I would have turned into a snarling beast (about three minutes after the pre-designated time of arrival). This evening he's wearing more conventional attire than on our last date. He looks really nervous. In fact, so nervous that I feel like sending him home to put the poor man out of his misery, but this is my chance to make amends for any erratic behaviour or incidents that may have made him a little cautious.

'Come in. Angel's gone out this evening so it's just the two of us.' I beckon him in, doing my best to be reassuring but sounding like a black widow spider with an ulterior motive. He smiles back at me, looking not unlike a cornered guinea pig.

'A drink of something?' I ask, again trying not to sound too sharky.

'Yes, please. It feels strange to be here sober.'

What the hell does he mean by that? Whatever he means, nothing is going to deter me from my goal this evening, even if I have to force feed him neat spirits to achieve it.

'I mean, it's really good to meet up with you like this. I'm just a little nervous.'

Bless him for that. I thought what he really meant was: God, you're a dog without mind-altering quantities of alcohol inside me.

'Don't be. We've already woken up together, and you've met my mother. Things can't get any worse than that.'

'That was okay. Well, the night before all that was great. Thanks for getting Angel to lend me some clothes. I washed them and brought them back, by the way.'

'Thanks. Angel was nagging me about lending her clothes to strange men I've just picked up. Not that she has to do it all that often.'

'I'm glad you picked me up.'

'So am I.'

Things turn out to be more relaxed than I could have

79

hoped. Just before he arrived I'd been having horror flashes of him turning out to be a psychopath Norman Bates-style, or of the two of us sitting in agonisingly painful silence. I am feeling so calm and confident I'm even surprising myself. I never knew I could have such *savoir faire* in this sort of situation. If I'd known it was this easy I might have racked up a few more by now. I am feeling pretty amorous; as my wine intake is increasing so are my libidinous urges, and the glint in my eye is becoming increasingly predatory. I am tempted to forget about eating and just pounce on him on the sofa but I contain myself.

He has one of those immediately likeable faces – open and smiley. And Angel was right, he does have beautiful green eyes. I could have done a whole lot worse, I think to myself smugly. Not only is he an extremely convenient antidote to a cheating worm of a husband, he is very pleasant in his own right. I am blessed tonight; it seems even my hair has given up its anarchic ways for the evening and is behaving itself.

He hasn't mentioned he's hungry so I decide to douse him up with a bit more wine and then start getting tactile. We have already shared a bed. Yet however cool, calm and collected I'm feeling, the actuality of tumbling into one again seems quite a way off. These sorts of things grow increasingly difficult as you supposedly get older and wiser. In my case I seem to have become older and stupider while my shame sensors have grown more sensitive, so I know I'll suffer more for my mistakes. We seem to be locked in a smiling, civilised mutual appreciation of each other, which neither of us is bold enough to break with a heavy handed pass. I've thrown personal space to the wind and I'm sitting so close I can name his aftershave, but we have not descended into a writhing heap yet. I am still doing Machiavellian sexual calculations in my head when I hear the familiar rattle of my door opening. Angel is back.

'Uma, get your slap on now. I've got the limo for the rest of the evening— Oh, I didn't realise you had company, sneaky! It's the quiet ones you have to watch, you know. Anyway, outside is a six-seater with leather interior and mini-bar facilities so it's a big improvement on this sitting room. Get yourself together and let's go on an adventure. You should see the driver, he is gorgeous, really nice. He's mine – you can bring yours along with you.'

There is indeed a large, white car purring expensively outside my house. Angel is in the mood to have fun and intends to take us with her. She is bouncing up and down in front of me in an over-excited fashion waving a big, fat wedge of notes. It could have been worse I suppose, we could have been caught *in flagrante* on the sofa. Or is the worst scenario never getting that far in the first place? In any case, I know that I always crumble when faced with boundless enthusiasm, and very few people can be as wildly enthusiastic as Angel when she is in possession of a wad of banknotes.

In less than five minutes all three of us are installed on the back seat and Angel is handing out little bottles of champagne like an inebriated air hostess.

'We are going to cruise around in this car until I cop off with the driver,' she says in that foghorn whisper of hers.

I have already noticed the driver taking the odd sly peep at her so we might not have to stay out too long, though his interest could be due to the fact that every now and then she keeps getting out tonight's wages and giving them a little flutter. Maybe my date will just think we're wayward girls from a rich family – or maybe not. As Angel and I start concocting lethal brandy and champagne cocktails I can feel my control over the evening gently slipping away.

We pull up outside a Soho bar. I feel a slight disappointment that we have actually arrived somewhere. As a child I was such a mixture of lazy and shy that I generally preferred the car journey to the places we were actually visiting. Now, as an adult, I won't be budged. I cite a well-stocked mini-bar as my cause for inaction and the fact that I never intended to go further than my sofa this evening. My chosen companion has been a bit quiet until now but he suddenly chirps up and states that he'll sit this one out with me. I would feel guilty if I was less drunk. And I know Angel's drinking habits well enough to realise that this isn't going to be the only bar of the evening.

'Okay then, you pair can sit in *my* limo while I go in on my own and have a little scout around. Should I ask the driver if he wants a soft drink or something?'

'That would be a very nice gesture.'

'Wouldn't it just.' Her eyebrows shoot up into that smirk of hers. There is, I have worked out, one smirk for when she is misbehaving, a slightly different one for when I am (which she has a lot less call to use), and a third, which is higher than the other two, for when it's both of us. It is the latter that she gives me just before she sashays to the front of the car and raps on the driver's window.

Mission accomplished. I watch in awe as he removes his chauffeur's cap, gets out and the pair of them walk arm in arm into the bar. Angel has a real talent for this. Her success rate in bagging good-looking men is on a par with that of a flock of locusts clearing cornfields. Thanks to her charms we're left alone, snuggled up on expensive upholstery under Angel's black fake-fur coat. I can't stop myself from thinking that this really beats the back of a Ford Fiesta. Not that the blacked out windows are giving me ideas or anything.

'You can't say that visiting me is uneventful.'

'No, I'd never say that. It's fun. Insane sometimes, but fun.' We clink glasses and knock back another deadly combination of liquor.

I was feeling fairly frisky at home but now I have the added aphrodisiac of a large car and leather seats. Downing the last few gulps from my glass, along with any inhibitions that managed to dodge the previous alcoholic onslaught, I plant a large, sweet, brandy and champagne kiss on his lips.

CHAPTER 12

The scrape of stiletto heel on pavement heralds the return of Angel. We have not been all that outrageous; nothing that would warrant having to sneak her coat to the dry cleaner's tomorrow, anyway. I am having a very good time, and as Angel hoists herself back into the car I can't help beaming. I keep thinking: 'I get to take him home!' I have his arm firmly clutched in one sticky hand, as if I've just won him at the fair. Things have reached the stage now where I'm pretty certain that he won't bolt before tomorrow morning. Angel and Paulo, the driver, also seem to have hit it off and she keeps pulling down his little window for a flirty chat.

We have decided to head for some new place in Notting Hill. I am not overly keen on the sound of it but I feel we really should accompany Angel somewhere as opposed to simply getting merry on the back seat. The bar we've chosen is a chrome and glass hell-hole, crammed with the attractive but dull crowd that flock like desperate lemmings to this sort of place. Tonight, as I'm in such a blissed out mood, I don't care where we drink, and I smile sweetly at the two mountainous bouncers that give us the onceover before waving us through. The bar is mobbed. Normally I'd just follow Angel who can always navigate herself to a bar counter pretty quickly if she has to, but even she's having difficulty making her way through the crowds.

We are stuck behind a group of about eight men, all huddled together in a clumsy circle clutching their bottles of designer beer. I notice that one, a small, pink-faced fellow is sniggering in a really unattractive fashion and elbowing his friend in the ribs, looking over in Angel's direction. I place my heel right in the middle of his foot and allow my whole weight to balance on it for a moment as I walk past him. I hear him whelp as I do so and I carry on walking, hoping that I can lead Angel into the midst of a less antagonistic crowd. I get very nervous in these situations; Angel has the temper of a tidal wave on a bad day and is easily upset by arseholes. I silently pray to the god who looks after transsexuals and their friends to keep the group out of our way. Gaggles of vacant people wondering where to go next means that I can't get very far away from the troublespot, however.

I can see the pink-faced man and his companions coming up closer behind us. Angel has definitely noticed the bunch of giggling boys standing beside her. The pink one sidles up to her. She's got her eyes firmly fixed on him now, her nostrils beginning to flare.

'Oh God! Piers, you're right, it is a bloody man! I thought these things were for real at first.' With that, he reaches forward and gives Angel's left breast an exaggerated squeeze. Fortunately, she has quick reflexes and she gets his balls in a Vulcan death grip before he has time to squeak.

'What about these? These little pips all yours are they?'

She is holding him so tightly his eyes are bulging. His friends are making their way over to join him. As they arrive, Angel lets go of him and turns to me: 'Doesn't he look different out of drag, Uma?'

'Yes . . . I'd never have recognised him if he hadn't come up and said hello.'

'See you at Thursday trannie club.' She plants a big kiss on his nose and gives him a wink. His face is pinker than ever. There is a momentary parting of the crowds after their little exchange and the three of us make a dash for the bar.

It turns out that Angel used to share a house with the imperious queen who manages the place. They'd lived in the same squat in Camberwell many moons ago. We are led away to a raised VIP area which is cordoned off from the rest of the bar with little velvet ropes and has the only chairs in the whole place. We are shepherded through like The Chosen Ones and given a whole tray's worth of free cocktails to keep us going. This is more like it. Angel has recovered from her little incident with Pinky and is making the most of the situation by lording it over everyone queuing to get to the bar.

By my third cocktail I have lost the power of intelligent speech. I am only able to grin wolfishly at The Man Who Hasn't Run Yet and hope my luck holds. Despite free drinks and the enormous kudos of being able to sit down when everyone else has to stand up, the entertainment value of the place doesn't last that long. We decide to return to our wheels (all six of them) led by Angel who is starting to pine for the driver, who had to stay with the car this time.

He is still there waiting patiently when we get out. Angel decides to sit in the front for our return journey so that we can have 'plenty of room in the back'. The truth is that this allows her to stretch out in the front (towards the chauffeur). It is a lovely blurred ride home, with the two of us curled up together in the back. When we finally alight at my humble East End terrace, there are four of us. Obviously Angel's front seat overtures have proved successful.

We remove all the bottles that are left in the limo's mini-refrigerator and make our wobbly way back to where it all started. Angel leads the way with the chaffeur's peaked cap balanced jauntily on top of her hair like a trophy.

'We are not empty handed tonight, girlfriend.'

'We're certainly not,' I say with a happy, drunken leer.

'Just don't leave him in the living room like the first time.'

'No chance of that.'

We start with the intention of holding a final soirée in the living room, but we disband pretty quickly, sloping two by two upstairs.

CHAPTER 13

I wake feeling completely wrecked, but my ego and certain other parts of my anatomy are blooming. It hadn't been the evening I'd planned; it had turned out even better. I glance out of the window and there's a badly parked limousine taking up most of my street and I feel even better knowing that things have turned out well for Angel, too. It certainly seems that all's well with her because I can hear her trademark cackle coming from the other side of the bedroom wall. I decide I am not well enough to get up for real and climb back into my warmer than usual bed to make the most of not having to suffer this hangover alone.

The atmosphere in the house is very cosy. Paulo, Angel's half-Brazilian friend, is topless and making breakfast for all of us when we finally emerge from my room. Angel is wearing her 'cat that spent the night gargling cream' smile. Paulo has to return the limousine to the depot soon but Angel has gone for a spin round to Tesco's in it. She has hit the jackpot this time – a chauffeur, lover and a breakfast-maker all rolled into one. He does some amazing things with eggs, milk and cinnamon.

The two men leave at the same time. After their departure Angel is left sighing around the kitchen.

'I'm in love. He's perfect. Isn't he the most beautiful man you've ever seen?'

'Definitely up there in the top ten. I'd go out with him for the breakfast alone – that was delicious.'

'His cooking skills are nothing compared to what he's like in bed. He was fantastic and he didn't run out of steam – I've hardly slept.'

'Angel, you're always having great sex. I'm ecstatic to have accomplished the deed at all, so please don't crow.'

'You did all right for yourself. Have a good time?'

'Yup. Most importantly, this makes me, in my eyes, definitely not married. I've managed to have a really good night with someone else. This means that my husband is toast, yesterday's toast.'

'We should celebrate.'

'We just have celebrated in style. Let's wait a bit and then we can summon up the same troop we had last night and do it all again.'

'But I've still got loads of cash left over.'

'And I have loads of work undone from last week. I have to earn a living in my own little way so you're going to have to hit the shops without me.'

Angel hates shopping alone. She hovers a while, hoping to distract me and change my mind. I know that due to the after effects of last night's alcohol I'm not going to get much work done, but at least what I do for a living is sedentary, unlike wandering the shops in the West End. I ignore Angel's entreaties and go into sketch mode until she gets bored enough to go off on her own.

When she's gone I get to lie on the sofa with a miniature bottle of red wine – part of our booty from last night – and contemplate my success. I've been less vociferous than Angel about my night but I am definitely pleased with what fate deposited in my bed. He is a great improvement on what fate flushed from there only a few months ago. The best thing about him are his lips; my ex-husband suffered from a Kenneth Branagh-type deficit in the lip department. Matt's are perfectly plump and excellent to chew on . . . even better to be chewed with.

I can see some possible benefits of dating a trannie: I could raid his wardrobe in times of clothing crisis; between us we'd probably never run out of mascara; *and* from my experience last night, he only looks at other women when he's wondering where they purchased their accessories from. It's also hard to imagine a man who spends the occasional evening in a panty girdle being mean and macho. Something to do with the fact that I have seen him in his feminine state makes me feel less vulnerable in the opening gambits of a sexual affair.

I snooze off the red wine contentedly, waiting for Angel to return. When I open my eyes, it's dark. My head is muddled and groggy and filled with confused half-dreams. It is well past the time that all the shops shut and I feel disappointed that she hasn't shown up yet. Often her shopping expeditions turn into mammoth drinking sessions and she gets home about six in the morning having left half of the things she bought in a drunken trail about the City, although these sessions generally occur when she has an accomplice in tow.

Now I can't relax. I am a natural born worrier. I keep thinking about the fact that Angel is alone with lots of cash and I have a really bad feeling. I'm not worried that anyone has done anything to her; I'm worried what she might have done to herself. I wrap myself in a duvet and make a camp on the sofa. I sit and wait, listening to cars pulling in and driving off, but no Angel. I keep hoping that she'll crash through the door at any minute.

I doze off again and am in a half-conscious state when the phone rings. At last it's Angel. She says she can't explain over the telephone but she needs me to raid her underwear draw and find the money she has stashed there, as well as her passport. Also stuff that proves where she lives. This sounds horribly like trouble. I crawl into the back of a cab after sticking a long coat over the old nightie I've spent the day in (well, the day starting from when everyone left the house and I could slob out properly). I've got all the documentation I could find, a large lump of cash wrapped in an old pair of tights and a pack of cigarettes Angel asked me to pick up on the way. Everything is bundled up in an old carrier bag. I arrive at the address I have scrawled on a piece of paper. It is somewhere just off the Edgware Road, which is not a good start.

At the scene of the crime there is an irate Middle Eastern man holding a bloodied handkerchief to one ear, a policeman, a rather messed up Angel and an awful lot of broken glass. There has been an altercation. It has somehow resulted in the angry-looking man being projected through a large, glass window (this man being the actual owner of the restaurant). Angel is loudly protesting her innocence but it seems that one of the witnesses who saw her push him happened to be the policeman. I go into over-earnest, hyper-polite mode to try and smooth things over but my scruffy appearance does not convince anyone of my respectability. After an hour of haggling, insults and my pathetic attempts at diplomacy, it is arranged that Angel will hand over four hundred pounds now. Then she and I will accompany the policeman to the station to fill out some paperwork. No charges will be pressed providing the balance for fixing the window is paid in full within two weeks. Otherwise Angel will face charges for assault and criminal damage.

Angel is incensed when we finally leave the station.

'I can't believe I handed over four hundred pounds to that arsehole.'

'You didn't have much choice.'

'But that was my laser treatment fund. I'm now destined to spend the rest of my life plucking hairs out of my chin with a pair of bloody tweezers.'

'You can save up again.'

'Yeah, like I'm known for my canny thriftiness.'

'Well, if you tried—'

'Phh! You know I can't save easily, it's impossible for me. I have to spend money. I'm doomed to have a chin like Desperate Dan for the rest of my life.'

'You should have pushed him through a smaller window, it would have been a lot cheaper.'

'Hmm . . . I wish I'd shoved him out of one on the fourth floor.'

Her spirits are so low when we get back that I don't dare enquire about the events that led up to the finale in the police station. I can't even cheer her up by reminding her of the beauty of her new Brazilian friend. A small gloom cloud has descended upon her.

'That's it! I'm sick of being the way I am,' she announces before we shuffle off to bed.

'What do you mean?'

'I'm sick of being a trannie, with people guessing when I'm out, or not knowing at first, then clicking and turning funny. I'm really sick of it.'

'Angel, most people don't question who you are. Only a few idiots ever give you any trouble. I'm a girl and I'd love to look as good as you.'

'You really wouldn't want to *be* me, though. You don't know what it's like. Anyway, if people are going to think that I'm a man I might as well go around dressed like one.'

'With breasts and plucked eyebrows? People are really going to stare at you then. You look beautiful as you are, Angel – you should be proud of that at least. There are a lot of people out there doing the same kind of thing that look nothing like the gender they're aiming at.'

I do my best to cheer her up. Angel is usually so exuberant that it's a shock to see her deflated; she is so good at being her fabulous self that I forget that sometimes things can be tough for her. I try to empathise as best I can but I know it is true when she says I have little idea of what it is really like for her. I know what it is to wish that parts of my body were different, but not *that* different. I've asked her before whether she'd feel better if she had the full operation, but for some reason she doesn't seem keen. I mention it again now as she is so dejected.

'I used to want all that but it's a big deal getting it chopped off, and in some ways I'd still be the same – I mean, it's not like I walk down the street with it all hanging out is it? Some people will still click. As for boyfriends, they'd have to deal with what I am anyway. An operation doesn't magically change anything. I hate being me.'

Angel doesn't look particularly convinced when I reel out the many ways that I consider her to be blessed, but at least she doesn't come down the next morning with a pinstriped suit and crew cut.

CHAPTER 14

For three long days Angel mourned the loss of her laser treatment fund. Once she recovered she reluctantly let out the details of that fateful night. It was a normal man picks up woman, discovers that she's still equipped as a man and then gets shirty, kind of tale.

The night has been forgotten by the time the final invoice drops through our letter box.

'I have to pay another seven hundred pounds to that jerk!'

'What?'

'He's invoiced me eleven hundred pounds in total, just for a bloody piece of glass. I could have had my tits done for that. He wants the money by the fourteenth – there's no chance of him getting it. My phone hasn't rung once in the past two days and none of my regulars are due.'

This latest blow is combined with the fact that strange things are happening in the bathroom. I have a sneaking suspicion that my plumbing is blocked by large, blonde fur balls. The bath hasn't drained properly for weeks and makes strange, strangled gurgling sounds when you try and empty it. I have a pathological distrust of plumbers that increases every time I actually use one, which is why it has taken me such a long time to register that something needs to be done. Angel has a contact. It isn't one of her clients, but someone who fitted out a friend's place. Faced with the alternative, which is a telephone directory full of dodgy Essex plumbers, we decide to call him. We leave a series of very polite messages on his mobile phone answering machine, which appears to place us at the end of a long line of people needing his assistance.

An air of dodgy plumbing and debt sits moodily over the household. Angel is furious about the letter. When the subject of window payment arises, which happens quite frequently at her instigation, she turns into that girl from *The Exorcist* and starts violently swearing in a gravelly voice. It was quite frightening at first but I'm getting used to it now.

I'm more concerned about the possibility of actually coming up with some way of paying Mr Khaledi. Angel is still indignant at the fact that anyone would even consider making her part with such a large sum of money for something she couldn't wear (such as silicon implants or jewellery). We both agree that as it was his body that did the damage then he's really the one to blame. The problem being that Angel already has a whole stash of disturbing the peace and disorderly conducts against her name so she's not a good candidate for convincing the Powers That Be of her innocence. From a public phone box, to prevent Angel letting loose Hell's Fury down the phone line, I manage to negotiate a slight extension of the payment date. It makes the skin on my tongue crawl to have to ask favours from that lecherous restaurateur. When he isn't being slimy he is contemptuous and snappy. I would have liked to explain to him that without my intervention on his behalf, Angel may well have petrol bombed his establishment by now, but I make myself bite my tongue.

I would never have believed that our saviour would come in the form of a genial, boiler-suited plumber from Deptford. We managed to wrangle our way to the top of the queue after Angel rang and explained to his answer machine the urgency of our need to bathe. This did the trick and he rang us back to say he'd be straight round.

Four and a half hours later he is installed in our kitchen only a few feet away from the bathroom in question, having a cup of tea and taking numerous calls from other desperate people. He keeps telling everyone he talks to that he'll be straight over, which alarms us so much that we sit guard on either side of him at the kitchen table. In a momentary break from the volley of calls he deigns to slip into our bathroom and check out the pipes. Just as I suspected, he comes back with a huge blonde hair ball; what I wasn't expecting was the large, flashy man's ring nestling in the middle of it.

'I think one of you lovely ladies is going to be very happy,' he says, waving the matted, bejewelled lump of weave at us as we look on in amazement. Angel's face suddenly brightens and she whoops merrily, jumping up to give the plumber an energetic hug.

'That's where it went!' she says triumphantly.

After we gratefully pay homage and seventy-five pounds to the plumber, he departs. Angel then fills me in on the history of the big, square chunk of twenty-two carat gold with four fat rubies and one large emerald sitting with fantastically bad taste bang in the middle. The ring, it turns out, is the property of the mystery client who always sends her a limousine . . . who is none other than the fat, northern comedian with big hair that was on television loads when I was a kid but was currently fading even from the B-list in the Hall of Fame.

'Not that one with the big grey hair and the funny walk?'

'That's the one.'

'No! I grew up watching him every Saturday tea time. I always thought there was something suspect about him even when I was eight. Why didn't you tell me that's who you were meeting?'

'I wanted you to suspect someone a bit more glamorous. He's not exactly a movie star, is he?'

'It's a lot funnier, though. Do you go out in *public* with him, and does he really walk like that?'

'I don't really see him walking around. He's generally on all fours and a leash during our little sessions.'

'It just gets worse. Tell me more.'

'He likes to be taken walkies by beautiful transsexuals wearing only fur coats.'

'My innocent childhood memories have been defiled – I used to have a badge with that man's catchphrase on!' The image of the pair of them is strongly imprinted in my mind. I'll never watch the occasional Christmas reruns of his show in the same light again.

'He's alright. Anyone who'll pay me one hundred and fifty pounds to take them out for a walk is okay by me.'

'So where do you take him? And how did his ring end up in our plumbing?'

'I used to give him a quick stroll in his back garden in Highgate but he became convinced that all his neighbours were peeping at him over the bushes so we needed to find somewhere else.'

'You've been walking him in my garden? We live in a back-to-back terrace! Our neighbours are going to start thinking we are really sick and strange.'

'They probably do already. I only take him out when it's dark, though. I let him do his business and come back in again after a few minutes.'

'What do you mean, do his business?'

'You know, like dogs do.'

'Angel! No! I feel sick.'

'Don't be so uptight. It's doing wonders for those lilies I bought you at the Chelsea Flower Show . . . I'm only teasing! I just take him out there and let him crawl about for a bit. If it wasn't for that little walk round the garden I wouldn't have this right now. After he's done his doggy thing he gets all Howard Hughes and scrubs himself with a nail brush and disinfectant. That's when this little beauty made its merry way down your rotten plug hole and landed in my old hair. He was ever so upset, kept poking things down there but he gave it up as lost in the end.'

Unappealing as it is, this does help to throw some light on Angel's professional activities. She is constantly claiming that she doesn't really *do* anything with the mishmash of men that pay for her time, which is something I find puzzling. She is always a little vague on this point. Now I can see that she provides more imaginative services; and with her smart shiftiness I can see how she manages to dodge the more taxing demands.

I would probably be more annoyed at the debasement of my very unsecluded garden if there wasn't the distraction of an ugly but expensive-looking ring.

'You could give it back to him,' I say without any conviction at all.

'You must be joking,' says Angel, her eyebrows shooting upwards.

'You're right, it's not exactly pennies from heaven but it's near enough. It is a really unattractive ring. Aesthetically we'd be doing him a favour by not returning it,' I say sagely.

Angel has already shot up the stairs in order to fetch the magnifying glass she normally uses to inspect her chin for hairs. She comes back and carefully examines the stones with the air of an expert.

'Do you know anything about rocks?' I ask, surprised by the serious level of concentration on her face.

'As a matter of fact I do know a little something about

jewellery. I used to have a boyfriend in the precious gem trade.'

'Now there's a surprise.'

'He taught me a bit about what to look out for, what something's roughly worth, that kind of thing. He gave me some nice bits and pieces as well but I've sold most of it.'

'So what's this worth?'

'Well . . . to anyone with an ounce of taste, not a lot, but if you add the cost of the rubies and this big beauty in the middle, I reckon about twelve hundred pounds.'

'Wow! That's not bad for something fished out of our bath tub.'

Angel proves to be spot on with her evaluation. After an animated argument she emerges from an East End second-hand jeweller's with twelve hundred pounds clutched firmly in her manicured fist. I realise that the difficult part will be getting her to hand over the cash. I can tell when she starts eyeing up my cleavage with a faraway look in her eye that she's daydreaming about a pair of DD-cups. I try to argue the case that avoidance of prosecution is more important than big breasts, but she's not convinced.

'I need breasts that suit my stature. Big ones.'

'You always look voluptuous enough to me.'

'That's because I hoist them up. Twelve hundred pounds and some clinic in Budapest and I'd never have to hoist ever again. They'd just be there – rock solid.'

'I don't think that would look so good on you. Your nipples are perfectly aligned at the moment. God knows where they'd end up after some bargain basement surgery.'

As it turns out, Angel blows the first couple of hundred of her stash before she has the chance to make her way to Eastern Europe. I console her on the way to drop off payment for the window that she still has enough left for a pair of silicone lips, but the journey from E1 to Edgware Road is punctuated by deep, heartfelt sighs from her side of the cab.

It has been arranged that I will deal with the painful business of actually handing over the money, but Angel insists on hopping out of the cab and coming with me at the last minute.

'Please let's not break anything else or do anything illegal at all,' I plead with her on the way in.

'I will just finish the matter in a dignified fashion. Okay?'

To my amazement that is exactly how it goes. She sweeps into the restaurant as if it were her coronation. Her face set in a deep scowl of scorn, she peels off the notes, disdainfully letting them flutter to the counter and loudly demanding a receipt. Then she mutters something unspeakable in Lebanese (another skill acquired from an ex-boyfriend) and majestically exits.

She does whimper a little on the way home, though.

'I can't believe I handed over the money to him just like that. It's your fault − I just don't do that sort of thing. I would never have done it if it hadn't been for you pestering me,' she says grumpily.

'That's why we are good for each other. You encourage

me to behave more like you and I encourage you to stay out of jail. That, my dear Angel, is the secret of our success as housemates.'

Later that evening, as if in acknowledgement of her acceptance of this, she sheepishly hands me what is left of her ring money, the idea being that I will operate a sort of temporary savings account for her by hiding it some place. I find the perfect spot that requires wriggling on one's belly to the furthest point under my bed, among various tightly wedged boxes of assorted strange objects I've collected over the years, and then slipping one's hand under the carpet. It is, for Angel, a physically impossible manoeuvre; she simply couldn't fit in the small space provided by the obstacle course of my junk, so her money sleeps safely under my bed.

CHAPTER 15

Our household is relatively quiet for a while. I force myself
to work on various illustrations I have been commissioned
to do. I have spent a few pleasant, commotion-free evenings
with some of my other friends, who seem very pleased that
I've broken out of my stay-at-home hermit shell. I feel
a little guilty about hiding away without an explanation,
but as just about everyone seems to be involved in their
own post-mid-twenties crisis they are very understanding.
Slowly, all the faces I have known for a long time are trickling
back into my life – apart from the obvious one.

My friends seem to react to Angel with a mixture of awe
and fear when they first meet her, the exact proportions of
which depend on what kind of mood she's in at the time.
They all think she's fabulous – albeit a little scary. I can't
blame them; it is only my close friendship and proximity
that prevents her from terrorizing me. Living in the strange
capsule that our household has become, I have forgotten

what a peculiar pair Angel and I make. Her idiosyncratic and largely nocturnal life is great to be a part of, but I recognised early on the need to spend some time with my more down to earth friends, just as she has friends to call on that are more inclined to misdemeanours than I am. She has two gay male friends, both called David, who always come round in a pair to visit her. They are both absolutely charming when sober, and hysterical harpies when not. There are times when I watch the three of them reel out of the house and wonder whether I ought to follow them with a tranquiliser gun. Miraculously, no real mishap ever seems to befall them . . . or they never get caught, anyway.

On occasions when we are home but still fancy some company, Angel and I call up our respective men friends that accompanied us on that limousine night and sequester ourselves in our rooms for the evening. It is a wonderfully relaxed arrangement.

I have no desire for another husband – or even to get too swamped by a new lover – but I am very content with my gentle, smiling male friend with the big motorbike, a collection of evening frocks and a ready willingness to share my bed when asked. When I got married I had the naïve and old-fashioned idea that my sexual horizons stopped at my husband and that was the way it would be forever. Now that I am free to launch my libido wherever I wish, there is a Brave New World feeling about my sex life. I have a second chance to explore, and navigating the well-toned body of my new lover is a very good start. He seems calm but keen, which is the perfect state for me right now. I am bemused by the ease with which our relationship has evolved, having been used to the furious power struggle of a marriage. It has all the fun (and more) but none of the aggravation that my last relationship entailed.

I am comfortable enough with him to spend occasional nights at his place, which is unusual for me as I'm very attached to home territory. During my early visits I searched his flat thoroughly to check there wasn't anything scary there, like plug-in air fresheners or stuffed animals. I also checked out his shoes – I don't mind the patent fuck-me pumps that he wears when he's in drag but I did need to have a thorough scout through his male shoes, just to ensure that there were no cuban heels, pointy toes or slip-on things with tassles. I learned the hard way never to compromise on footwear. I once dated a man who wore blue suede cowboy boots and I still regret it.

There was no evidence of anything strange in his entire flat, and in fact it was a lot cleaner than the house that Angel and I share. I find it flattering to be his confidante about the trannie heart that's hidden underneath his leather jacket. Being of a curious nature I am only too happy to poke around in his most private thoughts. Unlike Angel he is perfectly happy being a man most of the time; there will never be any hormonal enhancements, or worse still (from my point of view) any surgical deductions. He is simply deeply drawn to the temporary illusion of transformation into the female form. I don't find it at all alarming – quite the opposite in fact. It does puzzle me sometimes I must admit, but I am rather fond of harmless foibles – even psycho-sexual ones; basically, anything that doesn't involve children, puppies or blood letting I can deal with.

I receive the occasional frantic phone call from my erstwhile husband, who has a long list of duller, more unpleasant personality quirks, such as lying and cheating. Strangely enough my memory of him has faded so rapidly that I am always vaguely confused when I hear his voice. I'm not quite sure how to place him in my life; he seems to belong to a time that is far away from where I am now. My married life seems distant and blurred, like an old summer holiday that I never enjoyed, so that all the precise details of the less than spectacular events have been forgotten. I came across a few pictures the other day, quite by accident, of the pair of us standing outside Wandsworth registry office, our faces stuck into frozen, frightened smiles. I looked hard at the people in the photograph and tried to remember what on earth I thought I was doing that day, but the present has leaked into my memory so much that I couldn't make any sense of it. I wasn't sure what to do with the pictures so I buried them back under the piles of junk where I'd found them. I thought I'd just let them sit there for a while as a monument to my stupidity.

My marriage has definitely rattled my faith in my ability to reach sane decisions. Fifteen good friends of sound mind even sat and impassively watched me go through with it all. I must remember to question them as to why they didn't manage to come up with any impediments at the crucial moment.

*   *   *

We don't tend to receive unexpected male visitors; mostly they have an appointment. The arrangement that we have severely curtails Angel's working hours – generally to when I'm out of the house. Her vocation has meant I've spent a lot more time in art galleries or libraries, so at least it has been beneficial to my education.

So I assume she has forgotten to warn me when I open the door to find a short, plump, middle-aged Indian man in a long raincoat standing on our doorstep.

'I think you're after someone else. I'll just call her for you.'

'No, I am sure you are whom I'm looking for.' I look up in confusion at two big, dark eyes shining brightly behind thick lenses covered in raindrops. 'I'm sorry to just appear at your door. I meant there to be some communication first, but I'm here now. I so very much wanted to meet my daughter.'

Angel, who is standing just behind me, scarpers up the stairs, leaving me alone to deal with a dripping wet stranger claiming paternity.

'Gosh . . . this is unexpected. I suppose you should come in.' I never once thought that I might be tracked down by my father. I'm really glad I didn't just direct him straight upstairs to Angel's room. I sit speechless opposite the man whose genetic matter is jumbled up somewhere inside of me. I notice that there is a general air of bumbling nervousness about him – I wonder if it's possible that it's an hereditary trait?

It takes me a while to contact all the necessary areas of

my brain and inform them of what is going on. While this is happening he mumbles through a quick summary of the reasons for his absence over the past twenty-seven years. He had, I vaguely remember at that point, sent my mother cheques every so often, but as these had always been spent on the most boring things imaginable, like school uniforms and books, I had never once been the slightest bit grateful for his contributions. That memory is sufficient to allow a slight thawing of my reception. I am at a loss as to how I should respond to this darker skinned, plumper old man version of myself, though. I don't feel like being at all unpleasant or even unfriendly to him, but in my mind the image of my mother is hovering above his head with her arms crossed. Then he drops news that is even more shocking than his original appearance.

'As I have been a widower for the past three years, I returned to England recently to take up a post at City University and . . . umm, how shall I put this . . . your mother and I have been rekindling our feelings.'

What? My mother with a man is very hard to imagine but my mother and father 'rekindling' – that's impossible.

'She hasn't mentioned you to me.'

'We felt we wanted to check out the permanence of our relationship first.'

I am starting to feel a certain petulance coming on. My mother and I: now, that has been a 'we' situation since I was born. When did she and he become a 'we'? I can't believe that she has the affrontery to have a life I know nothing about – and with *my father* of all people. Betrayed by that Marks & Spencer-clad hussy formerly known as my mother.

He says he understands that it is all rather a shock for me, then scuttles off with a plea for us to meet up at the weekend for dinner. I'm sorely tempted to take Angel with me so we can work our way steadily through the wine list and give him a bar bill that alone will make up for twenty-plus years of absent pocket money. That will put the frighteners on my prodigal father. It feels very odd that he has flashed in and out of my life. I have the feeling that I should have asked a lot of questions of this person that helped create me, yet I am too flabbergasted to formulate any.

Angel is suitably impressed by the drama of it all.

'A long lost father! Has he got any money?'

'I don't think he's got millions stashed away. Anyway, if anyone's going to milk him of his cash it should be my mother. She's the one who deserves it. I can't believe the two of them are together again. It's too strange – things like that just don't happen.'

'I think it's romantic. I wonder if my dad will turn up next with a big bunch of flowers and a crate of Chanel for me.'

'You never know, perhaps it's the season for it.'

'I doubt it. He still can't quite get his head round the fact I'm not going to marry a nice Italian girl and make lots of fat babies with her.'

I phone my mother later on that evening to grill her over events. I can't quite bring myself to believe what's going on until I hear her primly confirm the facts. She is extremely coy about the whole thing at first, but I don't give up easily. As far as I'm concerned she has a lot of explaining to do. She gently points out in her clear-sighted fashion that I had omitted to inform her of the collapse of my marriage at roughly the same time her own clandestine affair was starting up. We talk for a long time.

'It was unexpected for me too,' she says gently. 'I never thought I would ever want to see him again in the romantic sense. We talked on the phone and wrote for a long time before we became friends again. Eventually I agreed to meet up with him. He'd changed so very little – apart from his girth . . . he was a lot thinner in the Seventies. It's hard to explain, but that's what softened me really. The two of us have been doing very well without him. Yet his life seemed to be so . . . static. He never really came to terms with his decision. He made the wrong move and didn't move on – but we did. To tell you the truth, I think he's missed us a lot more than we've missed him. Anyway, I'm the lucky one. I've had twenty-seven more years of knowing my beautiful daughter. I can't stay angry with him.'

Talking with my mother has helped a great deal to make sense of everything. It was a bit of a shock to realise that she has an emotional life beyond caring for me, but if I put petulance aside I am quite pleased for them.

We are to meet as a threesome at some nice old-fashioned restaurant where family dramas can be played out within the privacy of a secluded booth. I feel more comfortable with the idea of meeting up with him with my mother by my side, and I have to say I'm curious to find out more about my father. This arrangement cancels out a whole weekend of sin . . . but there is always Sunday.

CHAPTER 16

The pair of them are actually sitting there holding hands when I walk into the restaurant. I'm sure there must be a by-law that exists to ban such public displays of affection in the over-fifties. At least they have the good grace to look apologetic about it when I walk up to their table. I am very grateful to the thick wooden panels in which the table is enclosed for hiding away the extreme awkwardness that falls as I am seated. The phone call I had with my mother lulled me into thinking that I was more comfortable with the situation than I really am. Like three amateur actors who've all forgotten their lines through nerves, we sit and look down at the table in a bewildered fashion. The embarrassment is so stifling that even the friendly Italian waiter disappears as fast as he can after I sit down. My father finally takes it on himself to make an inept attempt at conviviality. It is so badly botched that compassion sets in and everyone forces themselves to play along with him.

Things improve greatly during the main course; I am actually starting to enjoy the fact that they both seem so desperately keen for my approval. Every time I look at my father he has his 'Please like me' Battersea dogs' eyes fixed firmly on mine. My mother, in her own restrained way, is looking at me with more of an 'I'd like some indication I'm not doing something really stupid' expression. Both of them seem nervous but I also sense a feeling of excitement. They are looking to me to provide some sort of validation of recent events. I am, just for this one evening, The Arbiter of Approval, and I'm being sufficiently indulged by both as befits my role.

This time I have a much better opportunity to study the round, nut-brown face of Rai Seshadri, my father. The shock of his first visit left only a macintoshed blur in my memory. I am shocked to see how similar we are. He has the same big, wild eyes that dominate my face. Even his hair is unruly in the same manner, with large, fat curls that don't seem to know which direction they're supposed to be growing in.

By the time dessert is dished out I can tell the waiter is puzzled by the change that has come about, and he's not quite sure that he's brought his bowls to the right table. My father has launched into an anecdotal story of one particularly shiftless student and the unsuccessful attempts he has made to instil some level of enthusiasm in him. We have all warmed considerably; there is even the occasional sound of very gentle, controlled laughter floating out from our little section. My father comes across as a timid yet fairly charming character.

118

Smart, yet totally lacking in suave manners. I cannot help but like him.

It turns out to be an enjoyable, interesting evening, despite the strange circumstances, and everyone looks very pleased with themselves as we emerge into the chilly night air and split up. I notice the pair of them go off very cosily arm in arm. It looks like even my parents are going to get some action this evening. I trip off home on my own.

I know that Angel is meeting up with her Latin love god in between his driving jobs, and my house bears witness to her preparation process. There are scraps of black chiffon-type things and upturned shoes strewn about the place, and a strong aroma of hairspray and perfume in the bathroom. I sit among the fall-out from her glamour and have a small nightcap before I make my way to bed.

The good thing about spending an uneventful evening with my parents is that I feel fresh as a daisy the next day, unlike my alcohol-ravaged friends. I am the only one in our house who is raring to go to the assignment we'd planned earlier in the week: the Sunday tea dance. This, I had been assured by Angel, is as camp as Christmas and full of raddled old transvestites being whirled around the floor by dodgy men in dinner jackets.

Our own dancing partners will not be wearing suits. After three painstaking hours' getting ready, Angel, Paulo and myself are done up like funkier versions of contestants in a *Come Dancing* competition.

My date arrives at midday in his leathers but clutching

three bags of the necessary drag equipment. I witness his entire transformation from tousled half-asleep biker man to bright-eyed, shiny-lipped vamp. The whole process seems to take forever and I thought I had it bad just having to run a razor over my legs.

We all look splendid. Paulo is, of course, as masculine as ever in a white tee-shirt that looks as if it has been sprayed directly on to his well-formed upper torso. We all bundle into the back of the limo, which is filled with the froth of our under-skirt netting. Angel had bought a job lot down Brick Lane so we haven't skimped on our petticoats. We probably could have fitted at least one person and a mini-bar underneath. We spend the journey determining who can manage the most permanent *Come Dancing* smile. Angel succeeds in holding the longest, cheesiest smile without blinking. We award her with the only little bottle of champagne that had managed to survive her trip out the previous night.

'Make an entrance.' Paulo holds open the door for us and we try and dislodge ourselves from the volume of each other's under-clothing and elegantly squeeze our outfits through the door. We do manage a grand entrance. We definitely impress the old codger at the ticket desk because he gives us a deep bow as we sweep in. There is only a small raggle-taggle group of trannies and their admirers in there, but they are a very friendly bunch. A tall 'girl' in a leopardskin catsuit takes us under her wing and introduces us to the regulars.

The place itself is actually a big, old Victorian pub, but

there are now pink and white gingham tablecloths and tiny vases of plastic daisies on the tables that are arranged neatly around the big empty space of the dance floor. The venue was probably once a very grand place, a fact that is attested to by the elaborately moulded gold ceilings and some beautiful original tiling behind the bar. Years of neglect has seen it fall from grace – like quite a lot of its regular customers – providing the most perfect backdrop for this sort of event.

We have missed the dance lessons so we have to ad lib a collection of steps we think could possibly approximate ballroom dancing. This is a wonderfully civilised, timeless way to spend a Sunday afternoon. We spin about under the enormous glitterball to all sorts of classic music that generally only old people would get to dance to. I even dance with a few charming elderly gentlemen with very straight backs, who know all the right moves and do their best to instruct me. It is a great shame when it is seven o'clock and they collect up all our glasses and shoo us out. Unfortunately we've lost our big white carriage; it had to be returned along with Paulo in order for him to retain employment. It takes us half an hour of flapping at the roadside until we finally make it into a black cab. The driver looks like Walter Matthau crossed with a Sharpei and spends the whole journey completely silent and stone-faced, glancing in horror in his mirror every few minutes to check that we are for real. We certainly are.

CHAPTER 17

I have now succeeded in achieving a large number of successful sexual encounters on different days with the same man. This is no mean feat in the Nineties according to all the single women I know. Maybe this kind of thing is easier if one chooses a guy who's into frocks (and I don't mean some faggy dress designer, which is never a good idea). I have already happily mused on the fact that it would be really hard for my lover to tiptoe away in the middle of the night. First he'd have to find my cotton buds.

Another good point that struck me as we foxtrotted the day before was that the man I was with, when he's out at a nightclub, is firmly encased in a pair of size 12–14 firm control pants. There's something reassuring about this. My ex-husband could have done with some firm control over the contents of his pants. That human reminder of just how cruelly fickle taste can be has been making great efforts to meet me in person. Foolishly he keeps calling beforehand to announce the fact that he's coming round, which means he's never actually found anyone at home (from my hermit days I'm a dab hand at disconnecting my door bell, and at Angel's insistence I have new locks). He should have taken a tip from my Amazing Reappearing Father and turned up on the doorstep without warning.

Now that I know all about their secret love trysts I have been bombarded with invites to join one or both of my parents in various activities. I sometimes worry that the pair of them have completely forgotten that twenty-seven years have elapsed, and expect me to turn up in a pair of frilly pants and some t-bar shoes. To prevent excessive inclusion in their hectic social schedule I have invented lots of work. It's not that I don't ever want to spend time with them, I just think that the dust should settle a bit before we start playing happy families. I have painted a picture for them of a desk full of towering piles of blank pieces of paper on which I have to draw to scrape together a living wage, which allows me barely any free time to spend skipping about with them. I've actually done this rather too well because now they're both concerned that I'm working myself to death in a no-hope career. We do spend some time as a merry trio but I find it all very strange. Slowly I'm growing more accustomed to having a father, but I still tend to think of him as a pleasant, bumbling academic with an uncanny resemblance to me.

Their latest topic of conversation is the possibility of making a trip to India for Christmas. The idea was my father's and he seems full of excitement about it, but I know my mother and she doesn't travel well. She has a tendency to go pink in the sun and is stubbornly queasy when faced with spicy food. In fact, apart from a school trip to France in her teens she has never been, or shown any strong desire to go, abroad. Our summer holidays were spent in my gran's back garden, with me eating home-made ice lollies and jelly with bits of fruit in, while my mum lay inside reading magazines. I can tell from the tone of my mother's voice when the subject comes up that she would like to be keen but really isn't at all and is simply waiting for the right moment to say so. She must have waited a little too long because suddenly flights are booked and she rings me up in a panic.

'Uma, I'm not going with him. I can't believe he went ahead and bought the flights.'

'But the two of you have been talking about going for ages. It would be an amazing place to visit.'

'Yes, but I didn't think he'd go out and arrange it just like that. I've thought it through and I want to go to a nice hotel in Bath for my holiday. I want turkey and cranberry sauce for Christmas dinner. Can't you go instead? It would give the pair of you a chance to get to know each other a bit better.'

'I don't know – I'm not sure.' It's wimpish of me but the very thought makes me nervous.

'Well he has made the journey all by himself before,' she says rather pointedly, hinting at the fact that there's more than a turkey dinner holding her back. Possibly she still hasn't quite forgiven India for gazumping her all those years ago.

It's not like I don't want to learn a little more about him. However, the idea of two equally awkward people forced into such an intense bonding process makes me uncomfortable. I don't exactly say no to taking her place but I drag my heels on an enthusiastic go ahead. I am adamant that she shouldn't be left behind, with only teasmaid and chintz for company in a Bath B&B.

Despite ranting to me about it, my mother is also finding it difficult to tell him bluntly she doesn't want to go. The situation is resolved when they turn up together one afternoon.

'Uma, we feel that it would be really nice for you to have a break. As it turns out, Rai was a little premature when he arranged our flights. He has since been reminded of an important conference he'd overlooked.' She's thrilled to have wriggled out of it without being branded unadventurous. 'There are two seats – as a gift from us.'

'Wow, but that's too generous, I can't accept that.'

'Yes you can. We can't use them and it would be much less complicated for us to simply transfer them to you and a friend. We thought that nice girl who lives here could accompany you. Angel, isn't it?'

I hear a quickly muffled whoop from the hall, where Angel has been pretending to tidy up.

'You were thinking of us two going together?'

My father, who has positioned himself slightly behind my mother, is simply standing there, nodding and smiling shyly. When he's left by himself for a few moments I get to question him a little.

'What about your family and things, isn't it going to be kind of scandalous if I show up?'

'I have very little close family left, I'm afraid, and in Gujarat where my flat is there are only some very close friends, some of whom I have confided in all along. In fact, these people will be very pleased to meet you.'

'Me *and* Angel? It's very kind of you, are you sure?'

'Absolutely sure.'

When my parents leave I go upstairs to find Angel going through her summer wardrobe; she's practically packed her suitcase already in her excitement over my father's offer. She falls on her knees when I walk into the room.

'Take me with you. Please, I am your best friend.'

'If I go I will take you with me, if you promise to behave.'

'I will do anything you say as long as I can come. Anyway, trannies are looked on as gods over there. They pay them to bless weddings or something.'

'I'm not sure that's exactly how it is.'

'Do you know how long it's been since I've had a holiday? I haven't been anywhere outside of England since a summer holiday to Rome with my family when I was twelve. That's a long time ago.'

'Okay, we both need a holiday. But promise me you won't get into any sort of trouble out there . . .'

'I promise.'

CHAPTER 18

I accept my father's offer after a short period of moral dilemma. I do feel a little concerned that he isn't fully aware that my travelling companion isn't quite the nice girl that she seems . . . although not concerned enough to turn down the offer. I just hope his friends are used to bolshy, northern transsexuals, in which case everything will be just fine.

Angel, for her part, is beside herself with excitement. She can hardly believe that I am taking her with me and keeps checking that it is really going to happen. She's already managed to sweet talk Haroun from next door into feeding her cat while she's away. Even her legendary drinking sessions have been curtailed so she can get some spending money together for the holiday. She is trying very hard not to get into any more expensive trouble.

'I thought you said you could never save, Angel.'

'I can save to spend. You can buy chandeliers out there

the size of your living room for next to nothing, and cushions and amazing screens, statues – all sorts of beautiful stuff. I'm going to take three empty suitcases with me and just shop and shop.'

'So you won't want to be visiting the local museums with me then?'

'Local markets, that's where I'll be going.'

'Just as long as you don't interfere with any naïve, young Indian men you might find there, that's fine by me.'

'I once had a really beautiful boyfriend, half-Indian half-Egyptian. He was gorgeous.'

'Angel . . .'

'Okay. No men, just shopping.'

Now that London has started the countdown to Christmas hysteria, the idea of India is increasingly alluring. Our flights are booked for the second week of December so we can boycott the bulk of festive events.

Since the decision was made, it has been the main focus for both of us. We only allow ourselves the odd spin out in the limousine with Paulo and we try to keep those evenings fairly tame. We have seen quite a lot of both Paulo and Matt as we've worked out that this is the most cost effective form of amusement.

The only really noteworthy thing to happen in the month of November is the arrival of my decree nisi and the consequent annulment of my marriage. I had grown tired of my ex-husband flapping around like a loose thread and finally got round to sorting out the necessary paperwork and legal stuff to officially make him disappear from my life. We met just the once before the whole process was completed and he looked crumpled and shocked by the speed with which I had moved towards an official separation. It was a far simpler process than I'd feared: as the house was bought by me and in my name, and as his salary is about five times the size of mine, we are both prepared to take what we have and leave it at that. When the papers finally come through I am more pleased with my organisation at getting round to it than anything else. I am left with a slight nagging feeling, like I've just failed an exam (but not an important one – General Studies or something) but on the whole it is remarkably anti-climatic.

I feel young to be divorced, though there is nothing particularly unusual about it. I cheer myself up by thinking of the young divorcee who lived three doors from us when I was a child and had always opened the door to the postman in negligee and mules. I can be like that now.

Angel has kindly bought me a country & western CD entitled *Great Divorce Songs for Her*. It features such classics as 'You Can't Live With Them But You Can't Shoot Them'. It will come in handy if I ever fancy hosting a line dancing evening for divorcees.

CHAPTER 19

The week before take-off finds us insanely excited. We have bought a variety of guide books which we pore over every evening. The only downside is all the injections we need. I've read the medical section of one of the guides five times over now and have a horrible feeling that if anyone manages to catch Dengue Fever or Japanese Encephalitis, it will be me. Angel can't be bothered to go to the doctor's for her jabs; she says it's bad enough having to wait around there for hormone pills, and she's not going to have needles stuck in her arm for no good reason. She swears that all that's required is to drink pink gin every night, and we'll be perfectly safe from everything. I'm not taking any chances, however, and have every possible jab for every conceivable mishap that could befall a hapless traveller.

'Anyway, a spot of dysentry wouldn't be so bad. I could do with losing a few stone. Maybe I could get a tapeworm over there. Then I could eat as much as I like and I'd just get thinner and thinner,' Angel informs me over breakfast.

'I think your diet and lifestyle would kill it off pretty quickly. You'd have to take it to tapeworm AA meetings.'

Yet we both conclude that there is definitely an up side to the more common ailment that befalls most travellers to India, and we're looking forward to coming back a lot lighter than when we left.

The last days are mayhem. It has been sixteen years since Angel went abroad and she's been on the phone all week calling up everyone she knows to tell them she won't be around over Christmas.

Despite the fact that our excitement set in early, we are still packing in the early hours for our flight which leaves at the ungodly hour of six o'clock in the morning. Fortunately we are unable to sleep, so we spend the last few hours stuffing extra clothes into our cases.

We arrive just in time to check in and search sleepily for the Air India counter. There is a long row of people which snakes through the middle of the terminal. It kind of looks like a huge conga with luggage. This turns out to be our queue. I force Angel to join the back and not sneak round the front like she wants to. We settle ourselves down on a pair of trolleys. Gazing drowsily at the line of people ahead of us I am struck by the novelty of being among whole families of sleepy people with circles under their eyes that are as dark as my own. It is my first stirring of cultural identity. As the lack of sleep and movement starts to hit us we end up in a kind of stupor, hunched over our piled up suitcases. About an hour later I start panicking as there still seem to be hundreds of people to check in and the flight is due to leave in a few minutes. I'm scared that we are going to be left in Heathrow.

Just as Angel is about to start a riot we are chivvied up to the counter and handed our boarding passes. Now I can relax a little in the knowledge that, providing I can drag Angel out of the Duty Free Shop in time, we will be on that flight.

We are the last two people to haul our hand luggage down the aisle. We are given the two seats nearest to the window so we both have to squeeze past an apprehensive-looking Indian businessman. We are handed glasses of water and Angel sends them back in exchange for two large gin and tonics. One boiled sweet later and we're finally in the air heading for our destination.

Air India is forgiven for the phenomenal queue due to its saving grace of showing us Bollywood movies. Neither of us has ever encountered the delights of Indian cinema. Happily installed with curry and beer we watch handsome kick-boxing, disco dancing, hirsute heroes annihilate hundreds of baddies and get the girl. I only like the good guys but Angel shows a marked preference for the beefy, moustachioed villains. The plots are completely improbable but even the bad guys are great dancers.

Our thrill on landing in India is tempered by the discovery that our connecting flight is going to be a lot later than scheduled so we have five hours to kill in a Bombay transit lounge. This is large, drab and painted a really unappealing grey-green colour, and everyone around us has an unnervingly resigned expression, as if they have been waiting there for ever. We find that there are three levels in the status of chair that can be found there; which one you get depends on the number of days you've been in transit. We walk past the comfy-looking reclining chairs, with my tall, blonde companion turning more than a few heads. Past the padded upright seats, which are also fully occupied, and right down to the end where there are tiny little plastic chairs like you get in fast food establishments.

Here we are forced to open up the bottle of Jack Daniels bought en route, as neither of us can face the idea of such an interminable wait without deadening our senses a little.

Two hours and half a bottle of Jack Daniels later we are befriended by a group of painfully shy engineering students from Bombay University. After whispering among themselves for ages, they edge towards us with much trepidation and start politely enquiring about our origins and our destination. At this stage we are so bored of moaning to each other about the delay that we are delighted to talk to anyone new. Though, as a self-proclaimed Protector of Virginal Indian Youths, I keep a beady eye on Angel. They insist on pulling out a camera and capturing our twenty-four-hours-without-sleep faces for posterity. That one will look nice in their album.

Eventually the impossible happens and our transit lounge purgatory is broken by the tannoy announcement that the final leg of our flight is boarding. We wave goodbye to our new-found friends and, dizzy from JD and lack of sleep, make our way on to the plane.

We both pass out and are deep in the land of slumber by the time we reach our intended destination. We are shaken awake by a plump, determined-looking, sari-clad air hostess, who has obviously started to worry that we aren't in the land of the living any more.

The thrill of arrival is lost in a dehydrated, sleep-deprived, almost hallucinatory state. We slowly descend the steps from the plane with the agility of an octogenarian. Staying awake long enough to pull our luggage off the conveyor belt feels like an effective form of torture. The worst thing, which only really strikes me as we make our somnambulant way through customs, is that we are being met by a friend of my father. This is almost as terrifying as the idea of another four-hour wait in a transit lounge; it will entail conversation of the 'trying to make a good impression' type and I'm only capable of a few dry grunts at the moment. My tongue is like freshly shaven wood and my brain has closed down all but the most rudimentary functions.

Waiting for us is a smiley faced, round gentleman holding a piece of paper on which my name appears in large black letters. He navigates us through a scrum of porters and installs us on the well-sprung back seat of a white car. I am too tired even to register the unfamiliar scenery that floats before my eyes on the drive from the airport.

Due to the lack of any evidence of an intelligent life force lurking beneath our half-dead faces we are dispatched pretty quickly to a large, cream twin bedded room. I'm too tired to even attempt to brush the whisky-eating plaque off my teeth and just collapse under a large tea-towel-textured sheet.

CHAPTER 20

When I first open my eyes I have forgotten where I am. The noises that float in from outside are enough to tell me I'm not in London. The window has bars rather than glass, which means that the sounds of the street seem that much more immediate than I'm used to. Laughter, babies wailing and a whole other medley of curious noises drift in. I sit up and focus on a large poster of a plump boy Krishna playing a flute. This helps me to remember.

Angel is still asleep, snoring heavily on her side of the room. I move as quietly as I can to the window. Outside there is a small green square of park. Standing in a group in the centre are an otherwise sober-looking group of Indian gentlemen following the lead of a white turbaned chap in bouts of hearty laughter. This, I'm to discover later, is the Laughter School, which is a great form of group therapy that is practised over here. I would love to see the same sort of thing in Regents Park with fat, navy blue suited businessmen clutching their bellies and letting out big 'haw haws'. The only audience in the park is a serene-looking cow that is mooching round in a pile of rubbish, chewing stoically on an indigestible old rag. I have arrived in India.

I know that Angel has the ability to sleep right through whole days so I leave her cocooned in the room and scuttle to the bathroom. There I can make myself look and smell approximately human – rather than the sewer rat that arrived here last night – before I have to face our host. Washed and conditioned, I'm a different person when I pad bare foot into the living room. The room is dark and cool with a beautiful, solid wooden sofa – the sort that my gran had before she discovered interest free payments at Leather World. It is a wonderfully relaxed room, and smiling down on me is a large picture of a dancing Ganesh, his elephant trunk waving about with gay abandon.

I am presented with a delicate floral teapot and a pair of bone china cups by the smiling friend of my father who has foolishly taken us under his wing. His name is Mitesh. He is round, jovial and smells faintly of leatherette. He tells me that my father's apartment is the one across the hallway but there are problems with it so it is best that we stay with him. The last bit of information he relays while looking at his feet with a sheepish smile on his face, which makes me suspect that the 'problems' are not as big an obstacle as he makes out. I have a hunch that the real reason we are tucked up cosily in his spare room is that he feels like a bit of company and doesn't want to miss out on the excitement of two overseas visitors.

Whatever his reasons, we are happy with the arrangement. He shows me around my father's place just before Angel manages to stagger out of bed and join me on the large wooden swing that hangs on the balcony outside our bedroom window.

It feels strange to wander through the dark rooms of my father's shuttered up apartment. This is where he lived with the wife his parents had chosen for him. Standing in that dust-filled flat I understand even better what my mother was trying to explain. There is a strong sense of suspension – of two lives that co-existed peacefully but weren't going anywhere together. The walls are bare and there are no interesting artefacts of the type that clutter Mitesh's shelves. It is far too static and sombre for the man I had met in the restaurant, trying desperately hard to entertain us with his stories. It has been empty for quite a few months but I do not get the impression that his absence has caused the place to change very much. I do not nose into any of the rooms that I sense housed her more than him. I respect her privacy, but a mystery father has to be investigated a little.

From the moment I arrived in India my mind has been full of questions about my father. I realised that in England, for whatever reason, I have not allowed myself to really think about who he is and what I feel about him. By taking this trip I have little choice but to start thinking of him, his culture and what it all means to me. I have to work out what possible place in my life he is to have. Walking about the apartment that he lived in while I grew up elsewhere I'm shocked by the huge knot of twisted emotion I feel. I sit down on the floor and cry fat, angry tears, the sort that would have been cried by a child who never quite understood why she was left. After a while I stand up, go to wash my sticky face and feel a hell of a lot lighter, if a little foolish. Then I get on with my quest to gain some knowledge of this man who is trying to restake his rather fragile claim to fatherhood.

I look at his terribly serious collection of dusty academic books and a large desk filled with tattered papers piled messily into different sized metal trays. There are two bedrooms, one much smaller than the other, which appears to have belonged solely to my father. Everywhere bears testament to two people co-habiting drily. I feel a far stronger proprietary air than I thought I would. Before I left England I had a sudden panic that when I got out here I would have a 'cuckoo in the nest' feeling. Yet somehow the surprise discovery that I am the only issue of both my parents has given me more confidence in laying claim to my father, and I look around for a while, trying not to pry too intrusively, grateful that we're not staying in this more spartan and doleful place. Then, when I feel I've gathered all I can from being here, I return next door.

Mitesh has demanded that we both call him Uncle. Angel and I readily agreed; neither of us can actually lay claim to such a well-disposed relative in that post for real. Uncle, for his part, treats us like a pair of overindulged nieces. More tea is brought out when Angel appears in her sunglasses, this time accompanied by a large silver tray piled high with

Indian sweets and cakes. I can only manage to eat one piece of a very sweet circle of green and white dough and a bite of something that is bright orange in colour; it tastes like shortbread biscuit made with five times the normal amount of sugar. Angel manages to shovel down quite a few, so I get away with not eating any more without it being too noticeable. What is wonderful is Uncle's *chai massala*, which is sweet and soothing and we manage to drink gallons of the stuff, much to his delight. We swing gently back and forth and watch people, rickshaws, cows and vegetable carts go past in the street beneath our balcony. Occasionally people from the street peep up at us curiously and we smile back at them.

I can tell, as Angel and I both rock contentedly on the swing, that every now and then our thoughts wander and we are transported to Bollywood heroine land; we'd be running through the streets in heavy gold jewellery, or dancing sexily with a flexible co-star. From our elevated spot we can sit in our floaty Roman Road, ankle-length dresses (bought specially for this trip when we realised our summer wardrobe was more suited to Ibiza than India) and watch the women next door at the Yes Madam beauty parlour at work.

We peer down enviously as glossy-haired young women pull up on their scooters, or immaculate women in pale saris arrive riding side-saddle on the backs of their husbands' Vespas. The best sight of the day is a cool, young man wearing big, dark glasses and a fiercely grumpy look of resignation, driving a motorbike. Behind him is a triumphant-looking grandmother sitting demurely on the back with a large basket. He is definitely less than happy about taking granny for her monthly chin wax.

When there is a lull in the stream of customers, we manage to muster up the courage to get our journey-worn faces down there and check ourselves in for the rest of the day. The girls who work there smile sweetly at us and try to contain their giggles. We feel a bit pale and bloated standing among the other few customers, who make much more plausible contenders for a role as a Bollywood beauty. We are saved by a stern-faced, attractive woman who is twice the height and width of all the other girls and who introduces herself as the owner. She obviously terrifies her staff as, after a few sharp words from her, they assemble themselves in straight-faced pairs and quickly get to work.

The problem with a beauty parlour is that although the theory behind them is that going to one is a fabulous experience that enhances one's self-esteem, the actuality is that for those people flawed enough to need a trip to the parlour, it isn't all that glamorous. Catching sight of yourself in the mirror having your pores steamed open with a freshly waxed upper lip isn't all that nice. They do give serious facials over here; they even harvest your blackheads by scraping what looks like a fat darning needle over your problem areas. We stick it out with great fortitude, acknowledging that pain and humiliation is nothing in the quest for Bollywood gorgeousness. We haven't come to India to sit cross-legged in search for the Inner Truth; we're looking for the Outer Goddess. I don't flinch even when they shovel my freshly oiled hair into a big, blue plastic bag and leave me sitting in it for two hours, looking like someone's evil grandma.

Angel has decided to have her hair dyed brown. This has terrified all the sweet-faced, gentle girls that have been attending to her and murmuring 'beautiful' as they run their fingers through her well-bleached locks. They really don't want to do it but Angel is fearless and absolutely adamant that she's leaving as a bashful brunette. It takes the ascension of the tough boss in the cerise sari, who finally nods her head and takes over proceedings.

In the meantime they all conclude that I'm suffering from hair loss, judging from the amount of frizzy curls they yank out in the process of trying to run a comb through the corkscrew jungle on my head. From their response it seems that Indian women have no concept of tangles. To combat this, they bring out an antiquated square wooden box. I am a little nervous when they open it up and I see what looks like a strange portable torture device from the 1940s but I let them carry on anyway. I am actually terrified when they start running the nozzle over my head and blue sparks fly off in all directions. Apparently this is meant to stimulate blood supply to the scalp but it could just be a punishment they inflict on messy girls who don't brush their hair often enough.

After four tortuous hours I'm disappointed to find that I look exactly the same, although perhaps a little shinier and redder of face. Angel, on the other hand, now has dark auburn hair, which means we are very slightly less conspicuous on the way back up the stairs to Mitesh's apartment.

Mitesh is waiting for us, having prepared some food while we were being beautified, and he feigns amazement at our stunning transformation. We love him – he's the best honorary uncle a girl could have. He's camp and flattering and he makes the most wonderful vegetarian thali.

'In India I am quite an oddity. I am still a bachelor at fifty-five, I live alone and I cook,' he informs us in his wonderfully grand BBC voice.

Angel and I have our own theory on Uncle Mitesh but his explanation for his bachelorhood is that he has been too wrapped up in academia and his parents had three other sons and a daughter to marry off, so they had plenty to occupy themselves with.

'With all my brothers' and sister's weddings and lives to interfere in, my parents have left me in peace,' he says with a chuckle.

At the end of the meal, he starts rummaging around in the bottom of a huge chest that sits in his hall. He proudly produces a dusty bottle of whisky that he has hidden in there. Gujarat is a dry state, a fact I only informed Angel of after we got here in case she panicked and tried to import half the contents of a duty free shop. When I sorted out our visas I did make sure we had liquor permits stamped inside our passports, but I never fully explained to Angel the reason why. Having been filled in, she is all the more impressed by the sight of Mitesh's illegal stash.

I pour out three measures gingerly. I want to give our

new uncle the idea that we are the kind of girls who can manage a few nips of whisky and reach only a heightened level of sociability; not the kind who will drain his precious bottle dry in no time at all and then stagger into bed after a rambling conversation, devoid of reason.

Commendably we manage to stay on the civilised side of drunkenness, though we do make a noticeable dent in his bottle. We make amends by bringing out our own alcohol rations and forcing him to sample the delights of Bacardi rum. Mitesh is obviously not a real drinker. He sips at a much more modest pace than we do and by the time we have cajoled him into trying the rum, his cheeks have gone pink. There is a great air of festivity; it is akin to those created in Christmas sherry-fests with great aunties.

Mitesh isn't all that good at being discreet, and I sometimes see flashes of fear in his eyes when I ask him certain questions. He seems frightened that he will somehow cause me offence or let slip something he shouldn't. In this merrier mood he is more open with his answers. In response to my enquiries he tries to explain about caste and my father's Brahmin status. Angel is fascinated by it all. She wants to know how non-Hindus fit into this status quo.

'They,' says Mitesh with a faint hiccup, 'are all untouchable.' Then he looks at us apologetically.

He's saved by our jet lag which descends upon us very quickly. We are forced to stop questioning him and bullying him to try another glass of rum and make our way to bed.

147

CHAPTER 21

We wake bright if not early and find our host has already
made his way on his bicycle to the classes he takes at the
University. But not without first leaving us a huge flask
of something he brewed earlier and a collection of even
sweeter breakfast things.

As we sup our tea on the swing we notice a whole family
of black-faced white monkeys with really long tails watching
us from a tree. I only spot one at first, and then I realise
that there are lots of them, all languidly employed in various
activities: flea-picking, branch-swinging, gentle squabbling.
They look far too relaxed to get up to any mischief but we
soon witness one of the many monkey muggings that take
place. A middle-aged woman with a big bag of what look like
small, very pale apples strolls past. A big brute of a monkey
lands heavily beside her and makes her jump and drop her
bag. He wraps both long furry monkey arms tightly round it
and after a brief tug-of-war he scampers back up the tree still

clutching the bag. The woman laughs at first, then, annoyed by the sight of a munching monkey nonchalantly tossing cores to the ground, she picks up a few of her damaged fruit and lobs them angrily at her tormentor.

Angel finds it so funny that she starts convulsing when she tries to contain her laughter. Neither of us notices a much smaller black-faced thief on the roof who swings down and lifts Angel's sunglasses from where they were sitting on the floor, and high-tails it back up the drainpipe.

'Cheeky bloody monkey! It's got my glasses!' squeals Angel.

'It'll probably toss them back when it realises they're fake,' I say before dissolving into laughter myself.

'Good fakes, though. They were brought back all the way from the streets of New York especially for me – from a street vendor just outside of Tiffany's.'

'Well it looks like they'll end up on a roof top in Ahmedabad.'

Angel takes the theft of her glasses very well, but her delight in our monkey neighbours has gone and they're now called 'the furry thieving bastards'. We find out later from Mitesh that they are the well-known villains of the neighbourhood and that all the doors on to the balconies have to be kept shut to stop them sneaking in as bold as brass when your back's turned and performing a spot of daylight robbery.

Today is our first day to really explore. We are feeling bold and rested enough to take our tourist selves around town. We have on clothes that we think sensitively cater to cultural sensibilities but we probably still look like a pair of Western tarts.

My father had apologetically explained to me that the place we were visiting was not exactly a tourist hot spot. It's an industrial northern town complete with chaotic traffic and pollution. There's a noticeable absence of sights worth visiting in our guide book, but we find that this is not a problem. It is not exactly like being in a European capital where you have to traipse around trying to find cathedrals and museums to visit. Here everything is different, and even a trip to the end of the street with the two of us squeezed into the back of a rickshaw is an adventure.

We are situated in the heart of the city. We didn't click at first but the long street round the corner from where we are staying is the Oxford Street of Ahmedabad, and if we walk the other way there's the late night market, so we are in exactly the right place.

Very close to where we are staying is the corner on which the rickshaw drivers and food stalls congregate. It's a hectic place with a strong smell of kerosene mixed with the powerful aroma of fried onions, cumin and coriander. We would love to try some of the things offered on the stalls but our host keeps us so well fed that we haven't sufficient appetite. We hop into the nearest rickshaw and, as we have no idea where we want to go, we just indicate up the street.

Being on the road here is like playing chicken on wheels: kamikaze scooter drivers swerve in and out, and the tiny metal cage of the vehicle we're in seems paltry protection from the big lorries with their cabins painted with brightly coloured flowers and patterns like gypsy caravans. They steam past, admonishing other traffic for daring to be on the road with long, angry blasts of the horn. It's a great way to travel, like being on a fairground ride only much scarier.

We decide to alight outside the Gold and Sari Centre which seems as good a venue as any to start. These places show you how shopping should be: sipping lemonade under a large fan while the most exquisite fabric is laid out on a semi-circular mini-catwalk. We finger everything appreciately. Owing to our novelty factor as Western women, everyone seems particularly anxious to help us find something that suits us. Dismissing us as too pale to wear such colours they sweep away all the lilacs, pinks and pale greens we've been fondling and show us blacks, dark browns and navy blues. They even tell me I have a wheatish complexion, which I'm not too pleased about but they assure me they do not mean it as an insult. I'd always thought of myself as olive skinned.

'We want the pretty colours,' we murmur petulantly to each other.

'Three solid weeks on a sunbed and he calls me pale,' says Angel plaintively.

I do see their point when they persuade me to let them demonstrate a navy blue sari lavishly decorated with a gold pattern. I look like I am encased in very expensive wrapping paper, but fabulous with it. I'm sold.

Angel takes a little more persuading before the keen staff manage to wind her up in a piece of pure silk. She plumps for red and gold. It is actually a Bridal sari, but as Angel says with a wink, 'You never know your luck.' I fear she may be losing her mind to Bollywood. I'll have to keep a close eye on her.

CHAPTER 22

We leave the Gold and Sari Centre with a carefully written out set of instructions on where to get the undergarments to complete the ensemble. We are to return to collect our perfectly hemmed and finished saris the next day. It feels as though we've been sent off on a glamorous treasure hunt. We trundle off on another death-defying rickshaw ride to a tailor who has been forewarned of our arrival by the helpful men in the sari shop who phoned him to say we were on our way.

Each of us has, in a separate little bag, the end piece of our sari, which is to be used to make the blouse to wear underneath. The tailor shows us a book which contains no less than thirty-eight different styles of neckline. I never knew that even in the realm of such a simple garment there was such a complicated range of fashion statements. Then there is the tricky decision of the length of sleeve to consider.

The tailor has to stand on a stool to find out Angel's upper dimensions. He is a short man, and he looks utterly amazed at the size of her. To our delight he announces that he'll have them finished for us early the next day. We are then directed to The Matching Shop which is where the petticoats are housed. There are hundreds of them in starched cotton piled high, in every conceivable colour of the rainbow. The man in the shop starts energetically tugging at some tucked right in the middle of a whole towering stack, and we watch in awe as he produces two of just the right colours, without setting off an avalanche.

As we flit from place to place we are followed by many pairs of bemused, inquisitive eyes; our novelty appeal is no doubt enhanced by our disparate height and high levels of excitement over everything. Since arrival I have been acutely sensitive to the response that Angel might receive here, but the people we meet seem to presume that she's a good-sized German tourist. We return triumphant, only a day away from a full Indian outfit. Mitesh is waiting for us, looking a little worried. He seems surprised that we have managed to find our way around even the simplest routes. He overfeeds us again, with an air of relief to have us back in the safety of his living room.

We want to see more of everything. The obvious destination for us now is the late night market which is only one stretch of massively pot-holed road away. I can tell that Mitesh feels duty bound to come with us but is flagging fast from the after effects of yesterday. Despite his wide smile and his assurance that he is not sleepy, his eyelids are puffy and he keeps yawning. For our part we are quite happy to roam free.

'They will definitely charge you more. You should really take someone with you,' he says, looking sceptically at us.

I am sure he thinks that we will run off to the market clutching all our rupee notes and come back with some crafty seller's rubbish. We try and convince him that we can hold our own out there in the marketplace, but he still makes us promise not to buy anything until we're escorted. He assures us that one of the tough old biddies from the block will come with us on our next visit. We make our crocodile promises that we won't purchase a thing and escape from his protective care.

It is much colder outdoors in the evening than we were expecting. We both held firmly to the simple notion that India is a hot country, and despite advice to the contrary from my father, we both refused to bring anything warm to wear.

We bump along the road with the same friendly rickshaw man with the protruberant teeth and the gammy eye who had given us a ride earlier, the wind whistling through the thin cotton we are wearing and our backsides bouncing up and down uncomfortably on the hard seats.

The make-shift stalls of the night market are set up either side of a wide stretch of suicidal traffic. Each one is lit up with precariously balanced oil lamps. We wander from one persuasive seller to the next, all showing their goods with frantic enthusiasm. Obviously years of hippy travellers to India have given them a warped idea of British taste.

'No, I really don't think I want that multi-coloured duffle bag. Thank you anyway.'

'Please don't unfold those tie-dyed bedspreads just for us.'

What surprises us both as we look at the mirrored cloth of the Rajastani is that so many of the Indian artefacts have been exported to England; just looking at the wares on offer, we could easily be browsing in a hippy stall in Brighton market. The skinny boys darting manically between us, shaking strings of gaudy fabric elephants under our noses, make sure we don't forget we are in India.

At the end of the stretch, where the light from the lamps of the stalls fade into darkness, there is a novel collection of animals covered in stretchy nylon tiger print. I am quite taken with a three-foot beast with his mouth open in a large growl. Considering that he seems to be made out of wire, newspaper and nylon he is remarkably tiger-like in the dim light. I really would like to take him home but I have images of me walking through Heathrow with the Asian equivalent of the Spanish wicker donkey, and good taste prevails; well, almost. We both feel sorry for the two curly haired brothers who thought that they were in for a big sale and we cheer them up by buying the only things from their menagerie that are relatively portable – large, round fans made entirely from peacock feathers with big golden handles.

I am ready to start making my way back but Angel isn't prepared to call it a day yet. She beckons our goofy-looking rickshaw driver who has been hovering around us protectively and demands to be taken to somewhere where she can drink a beer (I am still trying to explain the notion of a dry state to Angel). He looks rather alarmed at her request at first, and then, indicating for her to hush, he ushers us into the back seat and we set off down the road.

We are taken to a hotel in a large, crumbling white building at the far end of the main street. There is a broken fountain in the middle of the foyer which sits rather forlornly without any water under a dusty chandelier. Looking around at the state of the place I am really thankful we aren't coming here to eat. When the menu is finally brought over by a hospitable man in a brown tunic, we are instantly disappointed to see that beer isn't even mentioned. Angel calls him back and in that booming whisper of hers explains what she is after. Again, after an initial startled look, he scuttles off and brings back two large teapots. He indicates to us with a sly smile that he has brought us 'special tea'. It is slightly flat with a strong banana taste but it is definitely a form of beer. We raise our teacups to each other to celebrate our success. It is so much more fun drinking beer clandestinely out of a teapot that we decide that alcohol should be declared illegal in Britain to up the enjoyment factor. There is the additional plus point in that drinking beer from a teacup means we drink at a more ladylike speed. We have only put away two teapots before I have to drag Angel from the hotel when she starts flirting with a pair of bellboys.

We get back to find that our host has failed in his attempt to wait up for us. We tiptoe past him in his striped pyjamas and dressing gown, lying fast asleep, curled up in a ball on the sofa.

CHAPTER 23

We have yet to complete the Bollywood glamour trail and pick up all the things we have ordered. We retrace our steps of yesterday and collect all the necessary parts. Angel is bearing up very well under the interest that she is creating. When she is met by the persistent stares of a bunch of brightly beribboned schoolgirls with tight, oiled plaits swinging either side of their heads, she just waves at them sweetly and replies to their excited chorus of 'He-llos'. She even coolly ignores the group of men that hang about the rickshaw rank who watch her longingly every time she passes. Considering that the London Angel does not often countenance so much as a second glance if she's not inclined to, things are running very smoothly for us. It helps that she realises that we are a curiosity merely for being Western, so she is much less sensitive than she is on the streets back home. Even so, I do thank the gods occasionally that it's a dry state.

It is brighter and much hotter today and we are forced back to our balcony swing to eat kulfi and fan ourselves with peacock feathers. Having a balcony removes any pressing desire to travel about as there is constant activity right under our noses. Here in this dusty street just curving off the main promenade, life tumbles messily out on to the sidewalk. In the apartment directly above Mitesh's there lives a blind music teacher whom we have never seen, but we do encounter his sulky, unwilling pupils arriving and leaving; their shaky attempts at playing an instrument neither of us can identify drift down to us all afternoon.

We would very much like to try on our purchases. The men in the shop have helpfully given us a leaflet on how to wear a sari, and it looks deceptively easy; in seven simple steps we should be fabulously attired. It's way beyond us, however, and we end up unartistically draped in cloth, looking more like we've been debauched while wearing togas than elegantly attired in a sari. We have to wait until Mitesh pedals home from the classes he's been taking so that he can find us some assistance.

He fetches one of the sharp-eyed old dears from downstairs. She can't speak English but merrily chatters away to us in Gujarati. We nod our heads foolishly and smile because we don't like to say we can't understand. I don't know what we agreed to exactly but soon a whole gang of harridans descend upon us. They all pass comments in that cynical old lady way and we have no idea what they are saying. They do know their stuff when it comes to getting us wrapped up properly, though. They even safety pin us in place, which is handy, because I keep stepping on the hem. Angel was a bit nervous of being dressed by the neighbourhood grans, but luckily the starched, thick cotton petticoat covers up any surprises. There is one old lady that seems to be eyeing Angel a little sharply, but everyone else marvels at nothing more than her glamour.

The youngest and plumpest of our helpers hurries downstairs and comes back up with a well-worn tape and puts this on for our benefit. It seems we have started off an impromptu party. Mitesh hands out his wonderful *chai* and everyone else sits around us with expectant faces. It transpires that they expect us to dance for them. They explain with a smirk that if we wish to dress in an Indian style we should be able to dance in one. A pair of lithe young granddaughters are produced, seemingly out of nowhere, and to the great delight of a very large lady in a yellow and white sari they show us with a sway of their tiny wrists and a series of well-choreographed moves how it is done.

It is, I suspect, just a well-practised form of ritual humiliation of British visitors for their entertainment. We are forced to stand in the middle of the floor as every available seat is quickly taken. They crank up the bhangra a few more times as our cue for movement and we smile pathetically at our audience, hoping for a reprieve. None comes and by the second round of *chai* we are forced to throw personal dignity to the wind and give them what they want. Eventually, after much hilarity for everyone else, there is some shifting of seats and we are allowed to sit down, totally shamed maybe, but at least our co-operation has made us popular.

This whole episode has confirmed a theory I've always held: that the British are renowned for their absolute inability to dance, yet they are too polite to say no in the face of friendly requests for them to do so. This is why other cultures pounce so merrily upon us and delight in watching red-faced tourists jig about in an ungainly fashion.

Once the laughter dies down and they all tire of making Gujarati wise-cracks to each other, they disband and leave us, still trussed beautifully in our saris.

We have refused to be cooked for tonight. There is only so much overwhelmingly generous hospitality that I can bear before starting to feel like an over-fed leech, and so I have earmarked a suitable place to eat from one of the guide books.

Angel baulks at the last moment and has to change her outfit; it doesn't help that she has chosen bridal wear as her introduction to Indian fashion. Nothing would have got me out of my sari. I love the way I feel in it. The sari is about as flattering an outfit as a woman can wear. It fits all, and size of girth has nothing whatsoever to do with how fabulous you can look in one. You can also wear platforms underneath and no one can see them so it's much easier to pretend to be statuesque. All in all, the sari is about a thousand times more woman-friendly than lycra. Though the origami-like art of putting one on is quite hard to master.

We clamber from Mitesh's Ambassador, his retro-style car. There are loads of similar ones on the road, mostly in white and classically cool. I have to move with a lot more care than I'm used to now that I'm clad so beautifully.

Angel is suffering from a bit of a come down now that she's changed into jumper and jeans, but it was her choice.

The place in which we have chosen to eat is an outdoor, traditional-style restaurant complete with banana leaf plates, dancers and puppets. When we arrive there is a man dancing while wearing a huge papier maché head; he looks like a Maharajah version of Frank Sidebottom. We lie around on large rugs and watch him until greed forces us to go in search of empty banana leaves to be filled.

The concept of this restaurant is that a troop of waiters, each bearing one particular dish, will circle round and keep dishing out their wares until you really can't take any more. They manage four rounds before they defeat us. We are joined at our table by two affable Canadians who entertain us with their complete incompatibility. They make Angel and me seem like Siamese twins. One has the enthusiastic naivety of a cub scout leader (the kind that doesn't get arrested) and the other is as drily sceptical as a person can be. Between them they prove a great double act and they keep us well amused over our puris.

Afterwards, barely capable of movement due to the amount of food that's been consumed, we lie down again and watch lithe young things dance about. There is even a transvestite dancer, who does an amazing whirling dervish-type dance on her knees and keeps smiling at Angel in a sisterly way. The highlight of the evening is the puppet show, which is manic in true Punch and Judy style, with about a dozen madly squeaking puppets with long, extendable necks cavorting about violently for our amusement. The children in the audience don't seem to be enjoying it half as much as the adults, who are all cackling and hooting with laughter. We are too full to get up to any mischief this evening and allow ourselves to be driven back on the bouncy leather seats of Mitesh's car.

I really don't want to take off my sari at the end of the night. I'm not confident about my ability ever to manage to put one on by myself. I stand in front of the full-length mirror in the hall and look at myself for quite a while after everyone has gone to bed. I really do seem to suit a sari and I feel a slight flush of excitement at the richness of a culture that I now have a very real connection to. Eventually I unpin myself and sadly unravel all that beautiful fabric.

CHAPTER 24

Mitesh has grown worried that there isn't enough to keep us occupied. He is busying himself trying to help us plan to see more of India. There is the Sabarmati Ashram right here in Ahmedabad, but Angel refuses point blank to go.

'No way am I going to an ashram. That's where rank old hippies have sex with one another in between yoga classes . . . ugh!' Angel shivers at the thought of having sex with a hippy.

'You've got it all wrong. That's the ashrams set up for Western tourists. This place is totally different. Gandhi's lived there – it was his headquarters or something.'

Even though my knowledge of Indian history is limited to two hours of Ben Kingsley I realise that Angel is totally misguided on this one. But she just won't be budged, however hard I try and convince her. I could go without her – she has been very well behaved – but part of me is just a little too cautious to leave her on her own.

Apart from the Ashram there is only the Calico Museum of Textiles, and even I cannot muster the enthusiasm for that one. Instead we stay in and plot the next step of our adventure. My father was anxious for me to see some of India, and as he financed the flights I feel duty-bound to return with something to report. Part of me is quite happy to stay within the realm of Mitesh's care, *chai* and swing, but India is a very large place.

Mitesh has spent a good deal of time on the telephone organising some trip for us; we are keen to discover exactly where we are going but he has skilfully evaded our questions and promises that all will be revealed in time. We were secretly hoping that he had a lion sanctuary in mind, but after sweetening us up with freshly baked samosas he announces that he is driving us to the outskirts of town to visit my aunt; this one being a real aunt, the elder and only sister of my father. I had been made vaguely aware of the existence of this aunt, but a sense of foreboding tells me that she isn't going to be half as much fun as our pretend uncle. Why else would my father be so lapse in mentioning this part of our itinerary? I am curious to meet more of this branch of my family, but as the three of us climb into Mitesh's Ambassador I have a feeling of no escape and, judging by Angel's lack of banter on the way there, she feels the same.

It takes us nearly an hour to reach my aunt's neighbour-hood. It is obviously a wealthy part of town because there are wide streets of large detached residences with heavy foliaged front gardens and large gates. Mitesh is confused as to which one of the row of houses is my aunt's. He explains that it has been a long time since he has been here. We keep pulling up outside a house he thinks looks familiar, making our enquiries and then driving off again as they direct us further along the road.

At last we come to the right house. There are two peacocks sitting on the gate, eyeing us boldly and refusing to budge as we try and open the heavy, rusty catch. One eventually hops off and starts pecking at the rings on Angel's toes. Above them, sitting in a tree, a dowdy, brown peahen is letting out bloodcurdling screeches, while a forlorn-looking black dog breathes heavily and bares its yellow teeth at us.

A very old lady in white comes to the door and only a little way behind her is the woman that is obviously my aunt. Standing very straight in an emerald green sari with her salt and pepper hair tied back in a long plait, she greets us with a nod of her head and ushers us silently inside.

The old lady disappears into the kitchen and we are led into a long, bare room with a marble floor and a collection of mismatched sofas set in a square formation around a huge Persian rug. She sits down graciously in one corner and embarrassingly the three of us try and squeeze our rumps on to one small sofa which is positioned as far away from my aunt's chair as it is possible to be. Mitesh quickly relents and bravely moves to a seat in a more central location. The room is not well lit, but even with my sight I can make out the large dark eyes of my aunt darting hard, scrutinising glances at the pair of us.

Usually when Angel is nervous she orders herself a quadruple whisky and coke and becomes more Angel-like than ever. Today she seems to be trying very hard to sink into the back of the sofa. The questions from my aunt bounce formally from one end of the room to the other. As soon as my aunt stops speaking her mouth falls back into its deep set downward curve. She was obviously very pretty when younger, but frustration and bitterness have revealed themselves etched into the deep lines around her mouth and the permanent frown that sits on her forehead. She looks, I think even as I first sit down, a perfect example of someone who has eventually got the face that they deserve. I think of the smooth, round face of my father and that permanently bewildered expression he wears, and like him more than ever after experiencing the hard, withering gaze of his sister. Now and then she stares incredulously at Angel for a short while before asking me more questions. I'm immediately aware that my aunt has a far more suspicious mind than most of the people we have come across so far and as such is scrutinising Angel closely. She seems to have sensed that there is more to her than meets the eye. All my concentration is directed to being faultlessly polite. We have already covered what I do for a living and where I live, which seems to have just scraped past her approval.

'Married?' she asks, and I can see behind that downward smirk that she is fully aware of the answer. I look across at Angel in the pause that follows and she smiles back sympathetically with a 'wish we weren't here' expression.

'No, not any more.' I fail that question miserably. A glimmer of satisfaction ripples over my aunt's otherwise concrete face. Somehow I get the impression that she isn't too thrilled about having an illegitimate niece.

She gets up at this point and sweeps out of the room, returning with the old lady who is carrying a pot of *chai* on a tray. My aunt stands over us and flashes a picture of three very smart, healthy-looking young adults at us.

'My children,' she says proudly. I look with interest at the slim woman in the centre, flanked by her two brothers, with a shining shoulder-length bob of straight black hair.

'Asha's married to a lawyer.'

'What about *these* two handsome fellows. Are they married?' Angel asks, raising her eyebrows and throwing an exaggeratedly lascivious look. It is the only small mischief that she allows herself but it is effective.

The picture is snatched away from us in the blink of an eye and we watch my aunt's green sari shoot back to the other end of the room, the photograph of the precious sons clutched tightly to the folds of fabric covering her large drooping chest. You would have thought that Angel had just hinted at her desire for a threesome with the young men in question, instead of merely giving their photo a quick letch.

Mitesh keeps trying to interrupt my interrogation and bring the conversation around to lighter, more general topics. These attempts are all immediately quashed by the lady of the house and she effortlessly returns to her preferred line of questioning. She refers some of her enquiries to Angel, which makes me even more nervous. Angel is suitably evasive, but under my aunt's knowing scowl I

171

can tell that she is using up her small reserves of patience quickly. Mitesh finally responds to the pathetic, pleading looks that we've thrown him from the onset and, exclaiming surprise at the time, announces that he must take us on to one more visit. My aunt rises to see us to the door and we make stiff farewells. I am pretty certain that it will be my only visit. It is obvious that I've been called upon to be observed rather than acknowledged.

CHAPTER 25

Maybe it's the fear of having to visit any more less than welcoming relatives, but we decide that it is the right time to leave Ahmedebad and explore some more. Our first port of call, on Mitesh's suggestion, is to be the pink city of Jaipur. We are nervous yet excited about setting off on our own.

Mitesh, in the uncle role he does so well, is also fretting. He organises for us to be picked up by a taxi-driver he knows and whisked off to a large yellow palace that he stayed at nearly twenty years ago. It is wonderful to drive through the streets and goggle at the sights: the scraggy behinds of dusty camels pulling large, flat carts; ramshackle roadside cafés; and the beacon-like beauty of slender, young women clothed in a blaze of colour walking along the roadside with large, heavy packages balanced effortlessly on their head. Even in this one city there is a constant awareness of the vastness of the rest of the country that surrounds it; an understanding that just as life here sprawls so freely on to the streets, so does this wild patchwork of different places sprawl across the huge continent that houses it. To stay in one place would be impossible for a visitor such as myself, who is greedy to see more and eager to find out something about a country I have barely any knowledge of and which has been home to one half of my genetic make-up.

India has always seemed to hold a great fascination for the British visitor – the Empire, the Hippy Trail, the Great British Clubber. It is like one big acid trip without the need to take anything lysergic; nowhere else seems to provide such a powerful source of wonder, exhilaration, fear and even horror. The swirling reality of India cannot help but attack your senses. Even Angel is becoming aware that there is more here than just one large shopping opportunity.

We arrive in the pink city late at night and are installed in a long rectangular building that looks like a box full of yellow fondant fancies all joined together. This was a palace in the days when maharajahs donned handlebar moustaches, went to English public schools and thought it was great fun to chase tigers and wield over-sized rifles in their khaki safari suits.

It takes us a while to attract anyone's attention to our arrival, and we stand neglected in the driveway until a short, brisk man appears and whisks us up to our room. On the way we pass a huge mural depicting buxom Indian beauties in agile poses splashed sensually across a cream wall, their blouses cropped high above their round, brown breasts. It always amazes me the potent sexuality of a country that I'd grown to think of as prudish.

During our relaxed afternoons on Mitesh's swing, Angel and I had studied in great detail a copy of the *Kama Sutra* she had purchased, to see if we could pick up any handy tips. It is far more erotic than any modern day porn, but requires a lot more flexibility. The *Kama Sutra* could definitely teach *Playboy* a thing or two. I'd need some serious practice in the art of yoga before I could manage a lot of the positions, and the men must have been hernia proof in those days. We (or our unfortunate partner) would be more likely to end up in the Emergency ward than in a state of ecstatic sensual bliss if we followed the manual too enthusiastically.

Our room in the palace is a cool lime. There are two small canopied beds in carved dark wood with floral fabric coverings that look like antique cradles for adults set in a vast open space with a black slate floor. It provides a wonderful sanctuary from the bustling world inside the walls of the city.

Actually Jaipur turns out not to be as pink as we imagined. We decide that it's more of a baked orange, the sort of colour Angel's face goes when she's been a bit heavy handed with her foundation. We are only a short walk outside the main walls. On our way we pass a very plump, sumo-style man defecating in a rubbish-strewn corner; with bent knees he strains unselfconsciously as we go by, Angel's eyebrows hovering high on her forehead. Past a spit with fiery red chicken tikka just starting to char, we come to a crazed intersection with traffic whizzing past at all angles. Watching out for the bicycle taxis that wobble by dangerously close to our toes, it takes us a while to navigate our way across. The air is particularly pungent in this part of the city – a heady, dizzying smell of drains blocked by indescribable refuse. I spend the length of the street trying not to inhale. We reach a broader street lined by red-pink buildings that give the city its name. Sari fabric, huge cooking pots, spices, bright paper garlands of red and gold: the shop fronts on to the streets, giving the impression that the wares themselves are all jostling for attention.

Jaipur is a city full of grand palaces, but best of all is the wonderfully surreal observatory, the Jantar Mantar. Here, set up high in the city, is a collection of astrological constructions that would seem more at home in a Seventies sci-fi movie or a modern art museum. It is somewhere my father has frequently mentioned to us as interesting, and it is impressive if a little baffling.

By the time we return to the sanctuary of our yellow palace we are dusty and tired. There is a library that has been maintained from the days when the maharajahs still pretended to reign. The musty books are locked behind glass shelves to protect them from more light-fingered guests. It is very relaxed here with just an occasional member of staff peeping round the corner at us to see if we need anything. Even Angel's energy for adventure has been drained by her first real day as a tourist. We sit and drink cold Indian beer, pretending to be maharanis and watching small gaggles of tourists come and go. Two corn-fed Americans sit hunched heavily over a tattered menu and whine at each other over its contents – cheeseburgers are not easy to find here. Three squeaky clean middle-aged French women sit with maps and books and look very serious as they plot their arrangements. A lone Belgian male scuttles in and then scuttles out again before there is time for him to be intercepted by my travelling companion.

We have had our own plans made for us by the wonderfully concerned Mitesh. Tomorrow we are to be taken by another friend of my father to two of the hillside forts that circle the city. We are a little apprehensive but as he is a friend rather than a family member we are also optimistic. As we have been told it is someone from his old University, Angel has decided it is one of his students. She is hoping that my father's friend will turn out to be a fit, young guide. I am wishing quite the opposite.

He is just how I wanted him to be. A very *old* friend of my father's – with thin bow legs and a shock of wild, white hair. He provides a negative possibility of igniting any ardour in Angel. Kabir Nasir worked at the same University as my father and Mitesh for many years. I can just imagine the three of them talking late into the night, squabbling endlessly about intellectual matters and interrupting each other in their eagerness to air their views.

He catches us on the hop, having arrived a good half hour too early. I entertain him in the corridor as Angel finishes painting her face with her sun – and sightseeing – proof slap. He is very keen to educate us and rattles off fascinating facts at a startling pace. It is all a little too much for my brain at ten in the morning but I manage to absorb tiny crumbs of wisdom now and then. He has falsely assumed that I have a far greater grasp on modern politics and economics than I actually possess. I should explain that he would be better off on the topics of Bollywood stars and the price of silk, but I don't.

He is quite taken aback by my companion when she finally does finish with the bathroom mirror and makes her entrance. Her face is framed with a long scarf and half obscured by large, round sunglasses. She has not yet set eyes on our fabulously knowledgeable, if not all that fanciable guide, Mr Kabir Nasir, and she emerges with that glittering hope of the attractive and predatory.

Her appearance saves me from having to explain my exact views on some current political matter; Kabir is so flustered by Angel he forgets his question and hurries us along to the driver he has waiting to take us to Amber Fort.

It is a lovely drive past beautiful buildings set in the midst of large, smooth lakes, the histories of which are outlined so comprehensively that they drift into one ear and smoothly out of the other. Unfortunately, our guide is so nervous of the siren in the headscarf that most of the information is directed towards me; Angel gets to daydream by the window.

There are three elephants at the foot of the climb to the fort. Each one has elaborate coloured chalk patterns from their forehead to their trunk. I feel sorry for them having to trudge up and down the hill decorated like this, carrying tourists and their cameras. Angel tries to make me feel better by telling me that they could be trannie elephants and would therefore be happy being photographed all day long with their pink and yellow chalked faces. I'm not all that convinced; only human animals would be fool enough to really enjoy such a pastime. We have to take one up to the top nevertheless as I'm not totally sure that the spindly legs of Kabir will manage it up such a steep slope.

The fort is stunning. Just the building remains, which allows us to wander through empty rooms, to climb up on to turrets and to stroll through shaded courtyards without having to take much in other than the atmosphere that is enclosed by the ancient stones and marble. Advancing upwards, we discover the lavish multi-coloured mosaics and mirrored panels of the maharajah's apartments. From here the view is superb. We climb slowly to the highest point we can find to sit and look down on the city and watch it stretch out until countryside takes over. Angel hasn't once complained that she is losing a day of shopping, but then I would never accuse her of lacking in imagination.

We make our way down on the same gaudy-faced elephant. From what I have gathered of Indian hospitality I'm fairly certain that food will be on the agenda at some point. Sure enough, we are taken to a small, white cubic house en route to our hotel where we meet with Mrs Sarina Nasir. She is even smaller and thinner than her husband, with bright eyes half hidden behind spectacles and pure white hair. Five large silver pots are already on the table when we arrive, the aromatic contents of each one hidden under the silver lids.

Mrs Sarina Nasir is no less fond of talking than her husband, though she is a lot less scholastic and dismisses him with the wonderfully wifely: 'Take no notice of his nonsense' as soon as we walk through the door. She is full of sharp witted advice to help us on our travels. She blithely talks over her husband with tales of Ayuverdic massage in the south, crooks in Delhi and instructions to avoid ice-cream at all costs. We do our best to listen to them both at the same time and they seem pleased with the receptiveness of their audience.

It is starting to get dark as we are driven home. It felt really good to have such a warm welcome from the Nasirs, especially after the greeting my aunt had bestowed on me. Through his charming but slightly eccentric bunch of friends I'm starting to get a much clearer picture of who my father is and what he has been doing all these years. He's often mentioned as one of the characters in their anecdotes. At a push I might even admit to feeling the seeds of a genuine, deep affection starting to germinate.

Angel makes up for a whole day of cultural and social activity by speed shopping on our final day in Jaipur, taking me up and down dark, narrow streets barely wide enough for the three-wheel cycles that attempt to make their way along them. I inspect gems, sniff sandalwood and help Angel carry her assorted treasures.

We leave in the evening to travel overnight to our next destination. The plan was to travel to the lush lakes of

Udiapur. This fell flat when we realised that not all hotel palaces are priced in our range of rupees; our first choice was in dollars — a lot of dollars. Out of necessity we devise a new route and set off to a different palace over one hundred kilometres away on the edge of the Thar Desert.

CHAPTER 26

We leave early and doze for the first couple of hours, exhausted by the strains of commerce. The landscape is flat and unchanging and at first we are struck by the stark beauty of it all. After a few more hours we are lulled into a trance by the repetitive nature of the scrub land and look out in silence into the distance; even beauty can become boring after a while. I'm amazed that our driver can keep awake to swerve out of the way of the occasional on-coming lorry which speeds past us with a blast of the horn and wakes us up. As he can speak no English and 'thank you' is the only phrase we have learnt from the Nasirs in Rajastani, there is little conversation between the three of us.

By the time we arrive I've fallen asleep again. I wake to find us pulling into the courtyard of our next palatial port of call. It's nearly dusk and a whole extended family of bluish-white cows are lazily mulling around a water pump among the dust inside the palace gates. The place is astounding: vast yet exquisite, made from the most intricately carved criss-cross panels of pinky-beige sandstone. It is exactly how one would imagine a desert palace should be: topped with high domed turrets and exquisite archways leading on to mazes of steps up to mezzanine floors and long passageways; circular courtyards edged with huge, princely rooms, the floors and walls decorated in richly patterned tiles.

Travel has made us dopey and we just stand for a while in the courtyard and marvel at the magical sight of our palace, until we remember the practicalities of finishing our journey. Our driver's tired face prompts us to hand over a large tip. His sleepy face lights up with a beautiful bright smile when we pass over one of our larger denomination rupee notes to say thank you for getting us here in one piece. As we make our way under the arches into the palace, Angel points out that you would have to give a London cabbie at least ten grand to get a smile of that wattage in return.

We are greeted by a slim, good-looking boy in a pair of golden earrings in the shape of a flower with ruby petals. These cause Angel's eyebrows to raise but we are to see them on quite a few young Rhajastani men's ear lobes, so we soon realise it isn't just a camp quirk of his. We are led up a confusing series of stairs and through several doorways to the part of the palace that is the hotel; a whole wing on the other side is still inhabited by the maharajah's cousins and their families.

The room he takes us to has very high ceilings and two double beds. It leads on to a large multi-pillared chamber flanked by not one but three balconies; the largest is completely tiled on the floor and walls in tiny blue, green and gold tiles. There is a circular patterned silver table in the middle of it and two throne-like chairs just waiting for us to sit in and toast our arrival in a non-dry state. The bath is actually a bucket in a small ante-chamber but when you're in surroundings like this mod cons don't really matter. Angel and I feel we fit in perfectly with our five suitcases.

'Home,' says Angel, placing a bottle of Old Monk rum she managed to purchase in Jaipur on the balcony table.

We are too tired from our travels to make it up the hill into the fort of which we are nestled on the very outer edge. We position ourselves on the throne chairs, get our hands on a rumpled sheet detailing room service and watch the slender, young relatives of a maharajah going about their business. Later that evening we manage to drag ourselves up narrow stone steps into the rooftop restaurant. There we can see the solid round battlements of the fort we have not yet visited illuminated orange by the moon, like plump Hallowe'en pumpkins against the night sky.

We have had a week of the most wonderful Indian food and I'm ashamed to admit that we jump at the chance to order pizza and beer. I am craving Chinese food, but the two English girls that are leaving when we arrive warn us that we might find this menu's interpretation of Chinese a little strange due to the inclusion of more local spices. Still, we are happy enough just to get our teeth into melted cheese. The combination of such fantastic surroundings and ready bar service quickly goes to our heads.

By the time we make our wobbly way down the steep staircase we have befriended absolutely everyone on the roof: two friendly Dutch men of the hard-core traveller type; a charming carpet salesman from Kashmir; a local tour operator who was getting all set to arrange some lavish desert tour complete with camels, princely tents and several indulgent barmen with big ice boxes. We probably provided everybody with a good hour or two of entertainment before we had to wander through the various passageways trying to relocate our room. At least Angel comes with me and doesn't disappear to make love on a Kashmiri carpet as I feared she might at one point in the evening.

CHAPTER 27

The hangovers we are left with are a physical reminder of the benefits of illegalising alcohol. We don't feel very well. Outside is the hum of teeming activity. We can see through the beautiful archways of our mosaicked terrace: the lepers, the jewellery sellers, the ox carts and a ragged gang of children playing in a scene that looks like it's from another age.

We have to explore, but first we have to counteract the poison that caused us to be the jesters of the rooftop the night before. A room service deliverance of scrambled egg and Bloody Mary does the trick and by the time the midday sun is starting to do its worst we're out through the arches and off to check out some back streets and bazaars. Before we've made it to the curve of the street we have already been sold handfuls of tin anklets by beautiful, persuasive girls in bright saris of pink and blue, wearing heavy silver jewellery in their thick, black hair. We buy the ones made up of tiny bells, so for the rest of the holiday we walk about sounding like lost mountain goats.

We are invited into every shop we pass, and Angel, who has an almost unlimited capacity for shopping, obliges them all. After a while, hot sun, hangover and multi-armed brass goddesses are making my head swim. I find a path out to the external walls and perch myself on a cannon. This is the first time I have left Angel unattended, but I leave her merrily beginning to haggle down the price of a bag of amethysts so I think she'll be occupied for a while. I was born with an inbuilt inability to haggle – it comes from an inner cringing guilt that I seem to be able to feel with ease. Angel isn't afflicted with such a cowardly streak and has a no-nonsense hearty attitude to negotiation. She drives a hard bargain but she buys plenty, so the shopkeeper is generally beaming when she finally gathers up all her parcels and leaves.

An aspect of Angel that I have never seen before and that is to surprise me now, is her charitable side. I have always been aware that she can be a generous soul but charity is a different matter. I've seen her dismiss panhandlers with the line that she needs her money to buy her *own* drugs and alcohol. She has always held that being born with a body mismatched to her mind was a pretty tough card to start off with and she has never shown any sign of a remotely bleeding heart. However, when faced with the sight of a beggar whose one-legged deal makes hers look like a full house, she is unerringly kind with her rupees. I'm impressed by this unexpected element in her nature. She is not as hard hearted as she likes to pretend.

After her haggle for more shiny stones she finds me moon-faced, daydreaming, as I look down the hill at the small, square sandstone houses that spread out from the base of the fortress. She has been very successful with her shopping and unwraps all the little parcels to show me her treasure. Her lengthy endeavours have resulted in her acquiring not only the bag of violet amethysts but also a pouch of tiny pink rubies. Her eyes are shining as brightly as anything she has just bought. It occurs to me, mistakenly, that as long as her spending money holds out, she won't even have the energy to think about sex.

There is something else she wants to show me. She leads me down to a wide street that makes up the main square of the fort. 'Government Licensed Bhang Lassi Shop' is painted neatly on the side of a ramshackle wooden hut. I'm confused; it's unlike Angel to get overly excited over a yoghurt drink.

'Look in the guide book under bhang,' she says, sitting down at the one rickety old bench that makes up the stall. In the book it describes bhang as a drink made from the leaves of the marijuana plant. 'What's more, on that sign it says Government *Licensed*, which means I'm not doing anything to break the rules.' She says this in such a decisive fashion that I don't even try to argue with her. She quickly orders us two aluminium beakers of the stuff. I protest, but quite weakly. I have spent most of the holiday being sensible – and it is a holiday after all.

Angel wants to order two more.

'Wait a while, Angel. I'm not chasing you through the streets when your brain begins to melt.'

'My brain never melts. I'm having some more.'

'Angel, I've seen it liquefied on several occasions but that's on home turf. India is enough of a trip all by itself.'

I manage to temporarily delay things by nagging. Then I spot a shop of semi-precious gems that she hasn't inspected yet and steer us in that direction. The owner has only just managed to offload a dusty bag of moon stones when melt-down begins for both of us. Slowly but surely reality starts to feel a little blurry. The rest of our stroll down the hill is like a colourful version of that soft mint advert. The dream-like quality of the place is heightened. We wander down the streets arm in arm in a dazed appreciation of the beauty surrounding us, now quite immune to the sales pitch of the people we pass who are met with only sloppy smiles. Commerce is quite beyond the capabilities of the pair of us; we simply follow one slow, particularly beatific, hugely pregnant cow down the hill.

CHAPTER 28

We spend the next eight hours jelly-headed until we both start feeling drowsy and crash out. I have very strange dreams involving overweight cows and goddesses with jewels for eyes. I would like to have uncovered some greater understanding or mystical revelation in my hazy state, but I didn't. It is quite unnecessary to alter one's consciousness here. India stays almost exactly the same – or perhaps gets just a little more confusing.

Among the various people we came across before we finally made it to our palace refuge was the tour operator we have befriended. We had solemnly promised to let him escort us to the sand dunes and find a pair of unfortunate camels for us to trek on. He is dutifully waiting for us at the gates the next day, when we finally emerge at about two in the afternoon still looking clueless and sleepy.

We have to temper his plans a bit because of the state we are in; there is no way either of us could handle a night in the desert. We'd probably get twitchy at the sound of a grasshopper. We cannot let him down completely, though, so we agree to a two-hour trek at sunset which seems the most comfortable of our options.

At the required time we gather ourselves up and set off for the dunes. Standing patiently by the road are two men and two camels with saddles covered in brightly coloured, patterned fabric. There is a smallish dark brown camel and a much older-looking pale one with a bottom lip that droops heavily and reveals a full lower set of gnarled yellow teeth. We choose our rides according to our respective sizes and are led off into the desert. As we get closer to the sand dunes we are passed by many other camel-riding tourists. A large group of Indians riding in pairs are a lot bolder than us and canter past, while we are still getting used to the strange rocking sensation which constantly feels as though the saddle is about to fall off. The more camels we see the more I am struck by the idea that they are the only animals really on a par with human beings for idiosnycratic ugliness. There are all sorts of peculiar-looking creatures, all quite distinct, sitting along the top of a dune where various holidaymakers are waiting for a sunset. Despite the fact that it is hardly a deserted desert, it is a spectacular sight. The colours of the sky and sand at dusk, punctuated by the sounds of camel yawns, is an enchanting experience.

Two hours sitting on a camel is tantamount to serious exercise for us and we are starving. Back at the palace we are joined for dinner by the Dutch pair. For travellers they are both pretty clean-looking. Angel is very perky tonight, which generally means that she won't be around to say goodnight to. I'm loosening up a bit on my guardian angel role; they're Dutch — they're used to anything. I'm left with the keen, uglier friend. He's pleasant enough but I have a No Ugly Friend principle that I intend to stick to so I retire alone to our room.

CHAPTER 29

Angel is very pleased with herself. Young Dutch is only twenty-one. And her encounter has helped us shape the rest of our journey. They have already organised their onward journey to Agra – the home of the Taj Mahal – and as we haven't really formulated any sensible schemes of our own, we decide that their plans are as good as any.

We assemble two days later at a time that is so early that I feel vaguely nauseous. Any romantic notions I may have held regarding train travel are crushed as we enter the station. There are too many people, some really peculiar smells, and we haven't got a clue what's going on. I watch with trepidation the mad scrum that happens every time a train pulls in. I am starting to feel like this could be more of a problem than I'd imagined. I'm not sure that the pair of us have got what it takes to get ourselves and our luggage aboard. We are saved by two porters who for a small fee simply hoist our cases on to their heads and with the skill of Houdini manage to haul us on and find our seats.

There is some confusion over whether we have found the right seats, as by the time we move off, the wooden bench that we're sitting on seems to have double the number of occupants that it should. As the extra people are ticketless sikh soldiers, who are tall, well-built and with cheekbones so perfect they would make a plastic surgeon weep, we don't like to complain. Two of them, who look like they could be brothers, are the most beautiful men I have ever seen in my life. Angel and I simultaneously get out our sunglasses so that we can ogle them sneakily. We both have to stop after a while as drooling isn't becoming. The Dutch boys chatter on merrily, totally unaware that they have lost us to fantasies concerning warrior men with large cheekbones and long black hair down to their hips.

Those two soldiers do make the journey more pleasant. After they leave and the spaces they filled are taken over by wide-hipped old men with bad coughs we begin to notice our discomfort a bit more. Babies are screaming, people with what looks like the entire contents of a small shop get on and off, and there is the constant shifting of weight from one buttock to the other to ease the numbness brought on by the unforgivingly hard wooden seats; the journey takes a lot longer than we had calculated it would.

The station at Agra has a much denser crowd than the one we embarked at. The stench here is not just peculiar but down right unpleasant and there is a vast number of shockingly deformed beggars. A small child tugs insistently at my sleeve. I look down and see an old face thick with dust and dirt on a child's body, then I notice that one of his legs is swollen out of all proportion and that the foot on the end is like a big rubber glove filled with water, his toes jutting out at all angles. I quickly hand over some crumpled rupee notes. This is a long way from the glossy world of Bollywood.

We feel as though we've been travelling for about four days. Both of us now look very crumpled. At first we just stand in confusion on the platform until our bags are snatched up by eager porters and we have to hurry after them so as not to lose them in the crowd. All four of us cram into the back of yet another white Ambassador car. I can tell as we all clamber in that Angel is already starting to lose interest in her young friend. Her attention span can be limited in these situations. As the Dutch have been travelling for a lot longer and are a lot less overwhelmed by the surrounding chaos of the station than we are, we choose to follow them anyway.

We are given a perfect reason to part when we reach the backpacker hotel where they intend to sleep. I swear that the whole thing has just been lifted off the set of a low budget version of *Prisoner Cell Block H*. The first room they show us has no windows and sheets patterned with the faint ghost of stains that could not be boiled away. Our luggage is quickly reversed and put back in the cab, despite the entreaties of the owner who shows us three identically grim rooms in order to entice us to stay. Angel says a hurried farewell to her very temporary lover and we head off to find somewhere that won't depress us. We have to pass by the Sheraton and the like, which houses the better heeled tourist, but find a place nestling behind trees strung with multi-coloured lights along the same stretch of road.

This place has large windows, a big marble bath and a fuzzy old television that picks up Indian MTV. This is more like home. One added extra, which we discover only after we are getting settled and congratulating ourselves on a good find, is an army of mosquitoes. These rise up from behind the curtains and around the bath as soon as we are safely checked in. I am the sort of person who feels guilty if I tread on an ant, but mosquitoes are a different matter. As far as they are concerned I'm a heartless, deadly accurate killing machine. Angel joins in armed with a copy of *Vogue*. By the time we have finished there is evidence of a mini-massacre splattered on the cream walls. Despite the slaughter we can still hear high pitched zooms over our head as we try to settle down to MTV after we've washed away the filth of the past couple of hundred kilometres. My hair seems to be acting as some sort of grime sponge and is brittle with dirt.

Unfortunately, the marble bath turns out to be merely a showpiece, as there is no plug and no water comes out of the tap. I generously allow Angel to go first when two buckets of hot water turn up, as she managed to wilt spectacularly over the journey. The dust has congealed with her foundation and she looks intensely grubby.

We had noticed that the Dutch boys, being the six months on the road with no money type, had not tipped all that well in the hotel, and their food and service varied drastically from ours. We have taken heed of this, and determined not to incur any wrath that might result in tasteless food, manky plates and chipped cups, we tip manically at every given opportunity. This results in new things being constantly brought to our room. We end up with four piles of towels, twelve buckets of boiling hot water and large amounts of hot chocolate brought to us in a beautiful filigree teapot. We also have a man with a large copper kettle-type thing come and spray our room in an attempt to kill off those last blood-sucking pests still flying about. We regret this immmediately; the stuff pumped into our room may not have any effect on mosquitoes but it is certainly toxic to humans. We are forced out of the room by the fumes and have to leave the comfort of lying in bed watching MTV to hover outside, wafting the door back and forth in order to create a breatheable atmosphere. Not that clean air is actually an option in Agra. The traffic that we witnessed on our way from the train station made Ahmedabad look like Toy Town.

There is a lot of activity in the garden. A forest of fairy lights marks the spot where groups of people are starting to gather. We find out from our trusty room service deliverer that two wedding parties are being held here. Apparently it is a fortuitous day to be wed. Angel says that she is up for donning her wedding sari and joining in the celebrations, but she is probably only doing that to frighten me. Something tells me that we might find it a bit difficult to gratecrash this one. I'm perfectly happy to spy on the proceedings from where we are, which is well camouflaged with bushes so we won't be caught as uninvited onlookers.

A band starts up and wonderfully sweeping music fills the garden. Then there is the alarming sight of crowds of men carrying Darth Vader-style light sabres, but these are of the two pronged variety and seem to grow out of big flowerpot-type bases, all of them strung together with electrical wires. Behind them is a white suited groom wearing a garland of orange carnations on a plumed white pony. We're impressed; they really do know how to hold a wedding out here. It beats a couple of tin cans tied to the back of a car. The guests are certainly not holding back on their finery either. There is so much gold on display that it would make the flashiest ragga girl look like cheapskate. A lot of the women appear to be wearing half their body weight in twenty-two carat gold. There is a serious selection of brightly coloured silk cloth decorated with golden thread out there as well. I think back to Wandsworth High Street and an off-white suit and can't help feeling a little peeved. I doubt if I will ever be foolish enough to go through with another marriage ceremony, but if I did I'd want one every bit as glamorous as this. Young girls have already started dancing in a graceful, well-coordinated circle and there isn't a drunken relative in sight.

Eventually we are able to venture back to our room without choking. We can still hear the music faintly when the door is closed and I fall asleep to the strains of the sitar and the hum of things that suck blood in the night.

The next day, like all good if not original tourists, we head to the Taj, that great white wedding cake of a monument. It is the supermodel of the sight-seeing world – that's why it photographs so well. We are allowed to enter after Angel is sent to begrudgingly check in her cigarettes and lighter. It isn't quite as I imagined. I had for some reason always thought that the Taj Mahal sat in some vast desert garden far away from anything. It is actually set among the heaving streets of Agra, though it does have its own modest grounds. On entering the gates, we find it sitting right at the end of the garden, in front of a long rectangular pool, which exists simply to reflect its beautiful white visage. It simply doesn't look real to me. I find that it is too perfect, too symmetrical and simply too hard for my imperfect sight to absorb. I half expect it to disappear like a hollogram when we draw closer. Even when we stomp right up its white marble steps it still seems unreal.

Angel loves everything about it. She makes me take almost an entire roll of film of her standing in various poses in front of that large, white onion of a tomb. She is disappointed to find out that only semi-precious jewels are encrusted in the walls.

'Damn! I smuggled in my Swiss Army knife for nothing,' she says with a smirk. 'Only joking – I haven't done anything bad to your precious country yet,' she snaps after seeing a momentary flicker of fear run over my face.

'It's not *my* country. It's where my father comes from and I barely know him so I haven't got much of a claim to roots here.'

'You act like it's your bloody house, and I'm the sort of

guest that misses the ash tray and pees in the kitchen sink. You don't need to keep an eye on me all the time . . .'

'Well, neither of those actions would be all that unlikely for you,' I retaliate, stung by her allusion that I have been too quick to assume an affinity to a place I have no real link to.

Both of us grumpily lose interest in the Taj Mahal after that. We find a rooftop café where, set over the ramshackle disorder of the Agra skyline, the Taj – or just the great domed head that we can see – is much easier for me to assimilate. In fact, when it isn't in front of me I can picture it really clearly and can then marvel at its smooth marble perfection.

On the menu is a concoction called moon bananas, which we order; this turns out to be bananas nestled in ice-cream and coconut milk. After a very long wait they also manage to produce some dusty bottles of beer. In the meantime we have been befriended by the owner, Rahjan, complete with cell phone and shell suit; wide boys are universal. He's very interested in the fact that we live in London as he's heading out there soon to visit his sister. He pulls up a chair next to Angel.

I'm determined to follow a new *laissez-faire* policy. If she's interested in a man who owns a shell suit, so be it. As soon as I reach the end of my moon bananas I stand up with the intention of heading off and leaving her to it.

'Where are you going?' she asks, looking up from her cosy chat with Rahjan.

'I thought I'd go and do some more seeing of sights.'

She gathers up her things in a flash. As we make our way down the stairs she says in a whisper: 'Don't you go leaving me on my own – who knows what might happen to me!'

CHAPTER 30

There is no more babysitting on my part. Angel is now so frightened that I might let her loose that she sticks to me like rhinestones on a drag queen. I think she's well aware that she knows too little about this culture to get up to her normal mischief. There isn't any immediate call for it anyhow because less than twenty-four hours after those moon bananas we start to feel very ill indeed. Our robust health up until now has made us feel invincible as far as eating and drinking is concerned. We feel that the squalor of our own kitchen has probably made us hardier than those people who are more accustomed to disinfectant than we are. We are sensible enough to avoid the water but everything else has been fair game.

I am the first to fall. One minute I am bouncing about in a sleek hair-piece and floor-length embroidered waistcoat, all set for cocktails at the Sheraton, the next I am trying to shield my shiny new clip-on hair from splash black as I throw up.

A little later things progress even further so that I come to really appreciate the fact that the marble bath is in vomiting distance of the loo. I am seriously purged. Everything I have ever eaten seems to be exiting rapidly from my guts.

Angel offers some sympathy and then turns up MTV really loud to blot out the sound of me heaving. As we have a habit of eating off each other's plates so we don't miss out on trying anything new, I have a feeling that even if it wasn't those bananas, her luck won't hold this time.

Just as I dare to make it as far as the bed to lie down, Angel is starting to sweat, and I'm left in control of the television remote as she dashes to fill my place in the bathroom. It's my turn to pump up the bhangra. Luckily our policy of freely tipping means that we are well looked after in our infirmity by a constant stream of concerned waiters. This, combined with all the Christmas cartoons, means that it proves to be (apart from the occasional upheaval of the contents of my stomach) not that bad an affliction after a while. Angel keeps reminding me that we're losing weight with each heave, so that helps keep our spirits up.

Our Christmas day is spent, still a little wobbly and weak, holed up in our room. The real highlight of our day is watching *How The Grinch Stole Christmas* and the *Wizard of Oz*. Very late in the day we manage to keep down a whole lobster tikka and then tentatively start on a bottle of champagne that we have carried with us since Heathrow.

We end up spending much longer in Agra than intended. We had planned to spend Christmas in the nightclubs of Bombay, dancing alongside a breed we have so far seen only in the television ads – the Indian Yuppie. We now only have seven days left, and one of those has to be taken up with getting our feeble but more svelte selves on a plane and out of Agra. Angel is bemoaning the fact that after our illness we are pale and sickly looking. We have that grey-white look of too much television and no daylight. There is the tempting option of going down south where it will be gloriously sunny and we can recoup our health on the beach; or more likely trash it again at night-long raves full of gurning English people.

Northern industrial loses out to sunny south. Despite my better intentions we head to Goa. We are nervous about flying but everything we have eaten has stayed in place lately. All our travel plans have been made from the safety of our hotel room by our waiters who managed to bring somebody helpful in to make the necessary bookings for us.

Stepping off the plane at Goa we are hit by warm, clean air and sunshine. Maybe giving in to Angel on this one was not such a bad idea after all. I'm relieved when, at the taxi rank, we are allocated a really old man to take us to our chosen destination of Vagator. I reckon if he's survived this long driving on Indian roads he must be pretty good, though when he starts revving up the engine it occurs to me he may have taken this kamikaze job because he was too old to care. The south does seem to have a different pace to the frenetic buzz of the north; it immediately feels more relaxed. We make our way up the palm-fringed coast road revelling at our good fortune to be in sunshine in December.

The nearer we get to Vagator the more beautiful the

scenery becomes. The patches of palm trees get increasingly dense until we are driving through a thick forest of them. On the recommendation of our room service aides we'd managed to book ourselves into the only beach resort there. It is full of well-to-do Bombay families with spoilt, round-faced children. Best of all we have a little cottage which is right on the beach (though you do have to vault over a two-foot glass encrusted wall to actually get to the sea). There is an overhanging bush that is full of fat pink flowers and a sand-coloured cow looking very relaxed lying out on the beach right in front of us. It is quite a different proposition to navigating the sights and smells of Agra, though I am pleased that our trip has managed to encompass both experiences.

We sit on the verandah drinking rum, watching the sunset and smiling a lot. Behind our cottage, in a large open space, there is work going on in preparation for the New Year's Eve celebrations. Strings of lights are being looped around a large square fence. Huge metal barbeques and a red tented stage area are being set up. We watch with interest – this is where we will commence our end of year partying before we flag down a rickshaw and go in search of something a little less family orientated.

CHAPTER 31

Our constant cry all evening is 'Thank God we're not in London'; where, after a three-hour wait to be charged quadruple the cab fare to get someplace, it would turn out to be a heaving, sweaty mass of disappointment. Tonight, wherever we end up it will be outside in the very temperate Goan night air under the nearly full moon. Being rediscovered by a faraway father does have its benefits.

We are really going to go to town on our big screen Bollywood Queen look. This is one night that, with the general merriment and excess of the New Year, we may just be able to pull it off. Between us we have enough shiny clothes, fake hair and make-up to do the job of creating the sexy look of the mini-skirted variety of Bombay screen vixen. We start getting ready at six to give us a good chance. Angel is deliriously happy at the idea of being able to spend the next day comatose on the beach covered in olive oil, just to ensure that none of her friends miss the fact she's been away.

We turn up Indian MTV that has accompanied us most of the trip and sing along to our favourite bhangra tunes.

It takes us a fair amount of time to coax out our star quality. In the end we are bejewelled, bhindi-wearing, big-haired and essentially Bombay film goddess. In the area behind our bungalow on the beach, smart Indian families are gathering for the hotel celebrations. We can hear the DJ's ridiculous wedding-style banter filter through the bathroom mosquito net. It takes a little more courage of the rum variety before we tumble out and make an appearance.

Every group has been given their own separate tables – to the relief of the more sober families when the pair of us walk in. Our table is positioned in the middle of all the activity. After an initial period of mild disbelief, we are shown a great deal of friendliness, mixed with curiosity. These are the upwardly mobile of Bombay, and as such are keen to show off their cosmopolitan attitudes. We find ourselves being led off to the dance floor by tiny, giggling, bird-like teenage girls with grips of steel who encircle our table and implore us to join them; smiling sweetly they literally drag us from the safety of our seats before our drinks have arrived.

Later still we have the honour of being joined by their drunken middle-aged fathers, gyrating to rock music in a Tom Jones fashion. We are saved by the fireworks that are let off at midnight, which in the true Indian style of safety are exploded about three feet away from us; we spend more time making sure that none of the burning embers bury themselves in our flammable hairpieces than looking up at the display. Families are starting to disperse now and the DJ takes to the stage to host a bizarre type of award ceremony to keep the interest of those who remain. I manage to win the award for wearing the shortest skirt, which considering most of the competition are modestly attired in saris isn't the toughest of awards to win. Angel is miffed, thought. I collect it very graciously and everyone duly claps as I am handed my prize of vouchers for two nights hotel accomodation in a Madras hotel. I did notice that the man who received the next award for the least hair on his head received a heartier round of clapping than I did. I am still thrilled to win a prize – even though I give it away minutes later to our drinks waiter who seems keen to make sure my vouchers aren't wasted; there just isn't enough time left for us to make it to Madras.

This is only our warm-up celebration. We now have to find the other side of Goan nightlife; the side that is inhabited by the assorted detritus of European club land. We have been tipped off about a bar where everyone starts their evening and we make our way there by rickshaw. Here it seems rather a flat environment at first; everyone is either too stoned to speak or bunched into group and talking about where they have been or where they are going. Angel and I stick out in our shiny Bollywood disco attire alongside the more homespun hippy wear everyone else seems to be in. There appears to be a definite and complex status system of traveller, clubber, the most mashed of the Goan veterans, and so on. It is, however, a fragile set-up that will disintegrate later when little white pills make dancing muppets of most of those present.

People that we do talk to are very interested in how long we are staying; our three and a half weeks making us hopeless lightweight tourists as opposed to the hardcore shoestring travellers.

'These Indians, all they want is your money,' moans one particularly scraggy white male.

'Yeah, and all you want to do is keep it strapped round your waist you tight fisted bastard,' snaps Angel, voicing what I want to say but wouldn't dare.

We may not really fit in but we still want to party. There is the beach, which would be our first choice if our high heels didn't mean that by the end of the evening we'd end up buried ankle-deep in sand. Even closer is a party on a hill top, where we will actually be able to move our feet when we dance. We take the latter option and set off there immediately to escape the over-friendly attentions of a dazed-looking Mancunian drug dealer. The hilltop location is very user-friendly, with lights suspended from the palm trees that circle a large, flat plateau surrounded by white blankets from which enterprising Goans sell water, *chai* and other muppet-friendly things to very wide-eyed tourists.

The music was good; the setting, as we remembered it, was truly magical. We danced until dawn as blissed out as the rest.

The next day, when we eventually make it back to bed, we can still hear the faint throbbing of music coming down to the beach from the hills. We scarper just after we notice the first glimmer of the sun starting to rise – glamour and daylight do not make the best bedfellows and we are forced to scamper home and take refuge under big sunglasses and even larger sun hats. Having made it home we manage, after a short snooze, to lie out in the sun a few feet from our beach house until midday when we start to get very dizzy and in need of air conditioning and iced water.

I spend the day vacant but happy, wandering between sea and bed. This is the first time it has occurred to me that Angel is at a real disadvantage when it comes to swimwear. She won't go near the sea at first, until I point out a middle-aged Indian woman who is actually gracefully swimming in the sea in her sari. Once she spies this she feels a little less self-conscious wading into the waves in her shorts and long baggy top. It has been years since Angel has been in the sea and once she's in it's hard to get her out again. I can spot her head, still in shades and hat, bobbing about in the water far out from the shore. The sea at our part of the coast is quite calm – the only real hazard the beach provides is groups of fully dressed young local men who come on day trips to look on in astonishment and try and photograph the bikini-clad Western tourists.

We make the most of our last two days of sunshine. When it is time to take a cab back to the airport we can't stop ourselves from whining our protests at having to leave; neither of us is ready to wrench ourselves away just yet. We make a final phone call to Uncle Mitesh just before we leave, which deflates us even further as the reality of leaving is brought home much more by his entreaties for us to return to India and visit him again soon.

Once again we find ourselves in the same Bombay transit lounge with an enormous amount of time to ponder on the mystery that is the internal planning system of this particular airline. Even the Bollywood movie on the way back has lost some of its appeal, now that we are watching it while heading back to January in London. We sleep and sulk much of the way home.

Angel is alarmed at the idea that she may be made to pay duty on some of her booty, and spends the last few minutes of the flight transferring little bags of jewels from her hand luggage into her underwear. Walking right beside her I can hear a slight chink when she walks. As I have a face that assumes a look of pure guilt whenever wrongdoing is being done (even if I'm not the perpetrator) she makes me walk in front of her through the green channel. Sure enough I'm stopped and some old man is busy rifling through my dirty underwear while Angel breezes through with a carefree smile on her face. We are back.

CHAPTER 32

Arriving back, post-India, is like walking into a black and white film after romping about in technicolour. Everything seems grey and grainy, especially the people on the streets in their drab winter clothes. It doesn't help that it is January, which is as dire as it gets in London. It is a month of constant drizzle, dubious bargains and very little money.

I scan through my mail excitedly as soon as I get through the door; I always do this when I have been away, even though there is absolutely no reason why it should have been any more interesting in this particular three and a half weeks of my life than any other. I have one very meagre cheque for work done many months ago, loads of junk mail offering credit and the chance to win a car, and a handful of Christmas cards, including one from my ex-husband, strangely enough. How bizarre to have ended up as a name on his list of people to acknowledge once a year with an unattractive festive card. Worse still, it looks like I got one of the duff ones from near the end of his bumper pack. In small tight writing he asks if he may call round and pick up a few things he'd forgotten to take with him. There is an address and phone number printed in the corner but it's gone straight in the bin alongside the circulars. How difficult is it to replace a pepper grinder and an extension lead?

Angel has even less mail than I have and we spend a few moments scowling at a London that appears to have missed us insufficiently.

It takes us about a week to be absorbed back into our lives. By the second week my memories of India that I'm trying so hard to cling to are wriggling out of my grasp; it has become more like a vibrant treasured dream which brings with it a blast of powerful scents, colours and feelings. I can't seem to remember it as a whole, just fragments that are conjured up in my memory now and then. I have brought back a small sandalwood statue of a dancing Ganesh to bring us good fortune and the scent of this revives my memory more vividly than our collection of photographs, as well as alleviating the gloom of mid-winter London. Angel has a great deal of tangible evidence of her stay; she seems to have brought half of India back with her in the form of material goods and little bags of gems.

I have a long lunch with my father very soon after we get back. The whole meal is a kind of elongated thank you for my trip, during which I am anxious to say all the right things in case he feels he may have wasted his money on an ignorant daughter. He seems pleased enough with my responses (I am mostly honest but not always completely accurate in my account of our travels.)

'Mitesh commended me for having such a well-mannered daughter. Not that I can take any of the credit for that,' he says with a sad smile.

'He was the best as a host. We couldn't have been better looked after.'

'I bet he fed you too much. When I was first a widower he couldn't stop making food for me. He's the reason I got so fat. It is all his fault. Apart from Mitesh's cooking, which is excellent, how did you find India?'

'It was amazing – unforgettable. Thank you so much for giving me the chance to go,' I say nervously, in case he's expecting anything profound.

'One day we will go together. If you could bear to travel with an old man I could take you to some fascinating places you would not find in guide books. You can only have had a tiny glimpse of things in the time you spent there.'

I nod enthusiastically. Revisiting India sounds good to me, and next time I think I'd like to go with my father. Tellingly, he doesn't mention a word about my visit to my aunt.

It is our first proper meeting between just the two of us. There is a noticeable shift in the power stakes; it now hovers somewhere in the middle, with both of us seeking out the other's approval. I feel that I'm ready to start to accept him now that I have gathered a better idea of what he's about from my travels. He talks warmly about my mother. They still seem content with each other in a calm, middle-aged sort of way and I'm pleased for them. I am still not ready

217

to express huge gushing outbursts of emotion, but neither, I suspect, is he. For the moment a fond acceptance of each other is a good start. He seems in high spirits. I ring my mother after I get back from our meeting and she also sounds very chirpy. There must be something about revisiting the past that is giving the pair of them a youthful boost.

I am pleased to discover that sex and friendship are still on the cards with Matt. He appears unexpectedly and slightly anxiously one night soon after our return, not sure what his present status in my life is. I'm impressed by his lack of presumption and do not waste time ushering him into my bed. I am very glad to see him; even happier to discover that absence makes the sex even better. We devour each other hungrily, like eating ripe fruit. He seems to have missed me a great deal.

Angel's lover is not reintroduced in such a smooth manner. She rings him a few hours after we arrive to accuse him of adulterous behaviour while she was away. I'm not so sure that this is such a great tactic as she hasn't been an absolute angel herself on holiday. Paulo is even better at indignance than Angel. After a good hour of loud mutual remonstrations over the phone, she slams the receiver down in a fury and that is that.

CHAPTER 33

Everyday life has sadly returned. It is time to lose any Bollywood fantasies and get down to the unglamorous grind of earning a living. Commissions for illustrations slowly trickle in and I work diligently due to the lack of anything better to do. I want to return to India for a much lengthier stay. My desire to go back is so strong that it has stirred up a hitherto dormant ambitious drive. I need more work so I can afford the luxury of long haul travel. I'm so desperate to return that I force myself to tout my skills harder than I have ever done.

For Angel, January is a disastrous month work-wise. She slumps a bit without the combination of ready money and a Latin lover. When I first got back I bought a red flowered gerbera plant to add a little colour to the kitchen. Within two days all the blooms are looking at the floor. Angel isn't any cheerier. She has given up painting her face and slops around the house in a not-so-white dressing gown grasping a pair of tweezers. Most of the time she just sits in front of the television plucking at her chin. She's even kept her weave on well past the time when it needs replacing, causing her to moult; I keep finding lumps of old hair in strange places.

I offer to take her out in an attempt to perk her up.

'Angel, I've got some cash. You've stood me loads of times when you're flush. Let's just go to a bar or something.'

'I don't fancy it – I hate going out without any money.'

'It's my treat.'

'I don't want it to be. It is too much effort to shove a whole load of slap on and it's bloody cold out there. I'm not freezing my tits off for some boring bar or a club full of idiots.'

'Okay, I'll just get a couple of bottles of wine and a take-away. We'll have a nice night in.'

'If you like.'

She's not ready to be cheered up so I let her simmer for a while longer. I find that Angel is not someone who likes her bad moods tampered with that much. If she wishes to be down she will staunchly defend her right to be miserable for as long as she likes. After slagging off Paulo for a while she then starts to make herself into even more of a misery by going on what a wonderful boyfriend he had been before their abrupt ending.

'He was one of the few men that I liked who liked me just the way I am – you know, not funny about anything. He never went on at me about getting the full operation just so he felt better about being attracted to me. He was quite happy with everything the way it was.' She voiced this lament on more than one occasion but was far too contrary to even think of getting back in touch with him.

The two Davids come to visit her and are horrified by the lack of make-up and the state of her weave. They generally only see her when she's looking fabulous and is off out to create mischief. They try to get her to go out with them but even their persuasive hysteria has no effect. Angel is still sat on the sofa, tweezers in hand, when they leave early evening.

'What's up with her?' the taller of the two Davids whispers to me in the kitchen. I just shrug my shoulders, too frightened that she might overhear if I try to explain a bad case of post-Brazilian, no-punters, winter trannie blues.

CHAPTER 34

My work is starting to pick up but Angel's is still in the doldrums, although she seems to be chirping up a little as the British winter begins to thaw. One morning I find that she has woken up before me (which hasn't happened for a long time) and is out in the garden creating a lot of noise with some strange old piece of equipment.

'What the hell are you doing?'

'Making metal things,' Angel says cheekily, looking up, wearing a pair of goggles.

'Is that safe? Do you really know how to use that thing?'

'Derby Reform School for Boys,' she says with a smile. 'I was sent there for eight months once.'

'I'm not even going to ask what for.'

'Best not. It wasn't that bad there though, they taught us all sorts of stuff in an effort to reform all those delinquent young boys. Metalwork is what I excelled in – I always fancied making my own jewellery. I've got all those bloody jewels from India to do something with and I've had this equipment for soldering stuff for ages. I inherited it years ago when my boyfriend at the time got sent to jail; I think he's still in there so I might as well put it to some use.'

Reform school was not entirely wasted on Angel. A couple of hours later she proudly presents me with the first fruit of her labour – a snake with two pink ruby eyes; it is intended to hang on a chain and slither nicely upwards from my cleavage. It is a beautiful piece of modern jewellery – bold, over the top and very Angel. On the back she has seared a tiny, voluptuous, winged figure – her insignia.

She goes on to make three more creatures with pointy tales that are destined to spend their lives making sure that nobody misses the upward tilt of their wearer's cleavage. They are also great for hiding Adam's apples, as Angel demonstrates. Given the very nature of these creatures, they're bound to be successful and I enthuse wholeheartedly at each one I am shown. The next day she is out there for hours and makes a whole swamp of amethyst-eyed crocodile bracelets and comes in with her face smudged black with metal dust. For the first couple of weeks of her creative frenzy I am forced to rename her Sooty.

Together we traipse round various up-market outlets carrying her creations all wrapped up in tissue paper in a large polka dot hat box. Angel kindly provides some glossy black and white photos of herself modelling her pieces, which she wheedled a photographer friend to take, but she will only part with these in a tiny store in Bond Street where she has connections with the management. The rest of the less up-market places aren't worthy.

We manage to find a home for nearly all the pieces but Angel is sceptical about her prospects of making any real money.

'It'll take months to earn what I used to in an hour,' she pouts on the way home, after I hint at a possible permanent career switch.

It actually only takes one week. There is a triumphant cheer from the hall and she rushes into my bedroom to wave a cheque in my sleepy face.

'They've sold two already! At last I can afford to get out of the house. Please come out with me tonight, we've been cooped up here too long. Let's get dressed up and messed up!'

I grunt at her in agreement and try to go back to sleep. Later, when I wake up properly, I remember what I've done. Once Angel has solicited a yes to something she really wants to do there is no going back on your word. I am now bound under penalty of a terrifying trannie tantrum if I try and wriggle out of it.

My liver has had quite a peaceful month so far, though. It is time to wake it up in case it has forgotten the damage it will be subjected to for the rest of the year. As Paulo still hasn't been reinstated, we haven't got a chauffeur this evening so we have to suffer the indignity of going out on four wheels instead of six. The arrival of money has certainly changed Angel's attitude towards her little metal menagerie and she knocks up two more after she returns from her search for one of those 'Cheques Cashed Instantly' places.

Since our return there have been no big nights out. There have been a large number of small evenings in, but nothing that would entail escaping into an alternative glamorous reality. There is always a mixture of fear and excitement at the prospect of a night out with Angel that is a pre-designated bender. I can tell that she is bent on one hell of a night when she comes out in a gold stetson covered in sequin dust, impossibly tight gold trousers and an uplift bra. She's really making the most of the weight that she whittled away in India.

'Can you see my balls in these?'

'No, not really.'

'Then this is the outfit.'

Space Cowgirl is obviously her theme tonight. Being a secret fan of the greatest country girl of all, Dolly, I just can't stop myself from borrowing one of Angel's old blonde wigs and slipping into some trailer trash clothing myself. We've been too good for too long and it shows in the speed with which we start dusting gold glitter all over any exposed flesh. When dressed as extras from a John Waters' movie it is best to stick to drag or gay clubs and that's what we intend to do. Luck has it that tonight there is one of the best nights on for a spot of mid-week overindulgence. It is run by old friends of Angel's and she manages to catch them in and gain one of the essentials of our night – inclusion on the guest list.

We decide that it should be just the two of us tonight

as it has been a long time since that particular combination has hit London clubland. Matt shows up at one point in the afternoon and we make good use of him as a finder of shoes, brusher of wigs and waiter of drinks. He is then sent off home so he won't get in the way of us working our outfits. We manage to leave just after midnight, which is not bad considering that when it comes to being glitteringly glamorous we're a little rusty.

The club is located in some West End basement with a steep staircase that sees novice drag queens descending nervously, clutching on to the rail for dear life. It is lit just well enough to be able to see what everyone is wearing, and not well enough to see how such wonderful illusions are put together. Angel hasn't been here for a long time but appears to know or be known by everybody. I get a running commentary as we walk to the bar.

'There's Sydney, I hate that bitch.' They stop and air kiss each other. 'That one there in the big hat has got no front teeth you know, they're false – apparently she takes them out to . . . *you know.*' Angel starts miming fellatio with no teeth just after she passes the unfortunate person under discussion. There are a lot more similar jibes. Obviously Angel has been kept in the house for too long; she's had no place to vent her bile properly. Only a handful of people in the club meet her approval. The venue itself she loves. It is very plush in style – all over-sized metal chaise longues with dark velvet seats and dalmation-print fake fur on the walls. It looks like Cruella de Vil had a hand in the interior design. The people here have all made an

227

effort despite Angel's comments to the contrary. There are quite a number of gazelle-legged beauties sashaying around in extremely well co-ordinated little numbers. Angel's friends, who are supposed to be running the event, are nowhere to be seen at first. They are eventually found tumbling out of the ladies loo where they have been powdering their noses. They are both wearing fantastical creations in lavender velvet with two-foot trains trailing behind them that they are fiercely guarding from any stray, envious stiletto heels. They are wearing very high mink coloured wigs that are decorated all over in chandelier-type crystal drops. They are both using long pointy tendrils of ostrich feathers as false eyelashes. The original gender of either of them is not really clear; they are far too well disguised under all that glamour. They are friendly, irreverent and outrageously bitchy all at the same time. Obviously they were made to host nights such as these, and they sweep up and down the bar area meeting and greeting with a grand sense of propriety over all proceedings. By the very end, both of them are too out of it to actually stand up, and those mink wigs are starting to tilt precariously.

It is wonderful to be back in the surreal world that can only truly be found in the rarefied atmosphere of certain types of clubs. We stay right to the bitter end, loving every minute of drunken frivolity, exhibitionism and general disorder. Then, after helping the crystal wig duo make it up the stairs, we end up going on to one of those dodgy all-night drinking places in Soho, where the Maltese Mafia, prostitutes and starry-eyed clubbers tend to congregate. The feel of these places is very much that of a last-chance saloon in a cheap Wild West movie; both the truly fabulous and the highly dangerous can be found here but at that time of night it's hard to distinguish. Despite befriending all sorts of unsavoury characters we somehow both make it home unscathed at seven o'clock in the morning. We take our cab via the bagel shop in Brick Lane to buy a big brown paper bag full of fat cream cheese and smoked salmon bagels, to soak up some of what we've drunk and stem the tide of what we will suffer later from tonight's excess.

CHAPTER 35

That night out seemed to satisfy Angel's wanderlust for a week or two. It also put her in a sufficiently good mood to make a call to Paulo. His indignance at being accused of infidelity has long passed and he's round like a shot bearing a very large bottle of champagne as a peace offering. I scuttle off to Matt's for the evening and leave the two of them to make amends. It must have worked because when I get back home the smell of eggs and cinnamon is hovering in the kitchen and I'm pretty certain I know who made breakfast.

Angel is out in the back yard with her welding equipment and a big smile on her face. Her lover has already left, but judging by her look it won't be long before he's back again. She is still keeping herself busy making all sorts of wonderful creatures to adorn the wrists or necks of the discerning and the stylish. She has grown tired of her original collection of animals so I suggest she go on to mythical beasts, which prove themselves even more popular. The cheques from her various outlets keep appearing every now and then on the doormat. My own commissions for work have also started to look a lot more lively and I am beginning to witness an unexpected uplift in my fortunes. I get a call from someone I worked with three or four years ago who has an overspill of work and I am very happy to mop up some of her well-paid excess.

Surprising herself more than anyone else, Angel seems to slide into a monogamous relationship with Paulo very quickly after their reunion – overlooking any professional assignments, of course. Even her long-time ex-boyfriends whose names and faces I have grown accustomed to cropping up on an occasional basis late at night, seem to have bitten the dust during this incarnation of her relationship with Paulo.

Only a few weeks after his reappearance she declares herself *absolutely* in love. This is alarming enough in itself, but she has also started cooking. Paulo is an excellent cook and Angel never was one to be outshone. She is always capable of frying things to mop up the worst of a hangover but I've never seen any indication of more sophisticated culinary talents. Some days I'd be sitting at my desk scratching away at some drawing and Angel would appear bearing a plate of fresh pasta with some fancy sauce with more than two ingredients. Things haven't stopped there: she has moved on to fresh fish and *vegetables*. It must be the combination of Paulo and my more humdrum influence that has brought out the latent Doris Day tendencies in her. I'll come downstairs to find her wearing a yellow pinny next. Angel's natural diet as I was led to believe is: Marlboros, alcohol and take-aways. She puts it all down to the beginning of spring, but I think she could be overdosing on her hormone pills. Whatever it is, I'm seeing a hell of a lot less of her dressing gown.

Good weather seems to have come early this year and on some days we can both make the most of our freelance status with the aid of a large hammock we precariously manage to set up at the back of the garden. Angel made me test it first to see whether it would hold. When neither of us have any pressing work to do and the sun shines we light-heartedly bicker over who's going to lie comfortably suspended in the hammock and who gets the grotty old sun lounger that smells funny and sags in the middle.

My garden is unexpectedly green and pleasant thanks to the fact that all my neighbours' plants are hanging over the fence into my bit, giving the illusion that I have a real garden with proper plants, not just a few opportunistic weeds. This inspires me to link the idea of flowers and garden together. On the weekends that our alcoholic poisoning is merely mild we manage to make it to Columbia Road flower market for lunch and trays of hardy perennials just before it closes at two o'clock.

Angel loves flowers and buys herself huge prima-donna-sized armfuls and then growls at passers-by in the tightly packed crowd who are foolhardy enough to accidently bash into her bouquet. We eat fresh seafood from large polystyrene tubs and then stroll down to Brick Lane market to sift through the mixture of trash and treasure that can be found there. We are both fascinated by other people's junk and one of us will always come back clutching some curious find: a lamp made of plastic flowers, a hexagonal fish tank (that leaked) and our best yet – an original orange space hopper (that doesn't leak). The long winter months always make me forget the delights that an East End-based Sunday has to offer: rummaging through exotic blooms, outsize cacti, clay pots, second hand sunhats, big paste brooches with broken clasps and a whole carnival of strange objects crying out for recycling. Thanks to Brick Lane and its tempting trash the amount of clutter contained in my house is steadily approaching critical mass.

CHAPTER 36

One change has crept in to our lives with the onset of summer that is less welcome. Angel and Paulo have become completely inseparable, which in itself is not a bad thing. Paulo is undoubtably good-looking and charming, too. They are well suited to each other in an inflammatory sort of way (perhaps a little too well matched in the fact that they are very similar). Both of them possess an almost identical sense of humour and shortness of temper. The problem being that now that they spend every waking hour together the number of arguments resonating through the walls of my house has increased accordingly.

During the first few months of the year they were engagingly besotted, with only the occasional outburst of one or both of their formidable hotheadedness. However, as the temperature outside started to rise in the first flush of spring so did the tempers inside. They have the most phenomenal rows; it is like sitting through an opera, only with cursing and insults rather than singing. Half-Italian meets Brazilian in an explosive melodrama. I try and hide when I feel a storm brewing to avoid being drawn upon by Angel to join her side, or beseeched by Paulo to defend him on some point. They are both my very dear friends but I have begun to dream of them having their very own flat to shout at each other in. Paulo at present lives with his slightly unhinged, staunchly Catholic mother, so Angel doesn't tend to spend much time at his place. The arena for their arguments are the two storeys of my small house. They are the lucky ones; they're so involved in their quarrelling they don't have to sit and listen to it.

My own relationship with Matt seems supernaturally quiet in comparison. He is naturally quite a peaceful person. And I have learned from my one failed marriage that drama is not a necessary ingredient of my love life. What I require is tranquility and trust – interrupted occasionally with fantastic sex. This is my optimum arrangement. It seems to be working quite well, apart from the times I grow restless waiting for him to finish his lengthy transformation process from boy to babe before we go out for the evening. I don't mind in the slightest his slipping into a frock, I just wish it didn't take him three hours to achieve the desired effect. I have tried to teach him some speedy short cuts, but I think I may be missing the point a little. He seems to have a much more painstaking and ritualistic approach to glamour than I do, which I think must be part and parcel of the pleasure of switching sex. Despite my lack of patience I'm still not going to swap him for a more sartorially swift man; when we do finally make it out of the house we tend to have a great deal of fun. He is surprisingly companionable for a man, and equally so as a woman. I have ceased to worry too much about what, if any, implications his quirkier dressing habits may have and I simply let myself enjoy our unconventionally good relationship.

I would never have suggested moving out to Angel directly but when she brings up the idea one day I try to muffle my real enthusiasm while at the same time making it very clear that I have no objections.

'Now I'm getting money from making the jewellery it wouldn't matter that I couldn't do much of the other type of work,' she muses to me one day. 'I wouldn't want to just bugger off and leave you on your own, though.'

'Angel, I'd manage. If you want to find your own place, just the two of you, I'd be pleased for you.'

'I do get on really well with Paulo and between us we could probably manage to rent somewhere quite nice,' Angel says, without pausing to think too much about the accuracy of the statement.

It must have been fate, as a friend of hers suddenly announces that they are moving out of a warehouse-type place near Old Street. The pair of them discuss the notion heatedly for a long time and I eavesdrop with feigned disinterest. They eventually manage to agree that it would be a good idea. Angel is really excited when she comes back from investigating the place. It will provide her with a vast empty space to fill and a big flat roof for her overweight Persian cat to prowl around on without being bullied by hardier less inbred cats (which has been a problem in my East End garden). The size and emptiness of her potential new home will also provide her with many happy days of shopping opportunities. From her very first peep at the place she has started to devise elaborate plans for how she would like it to be. There's to be a tented ceiling and cushioned platformed seating area – a sort of vast 'Moroccan come Rajastani come Bedouin tent' boudoir. It will also mean that she will have the room to unpack her purchases from India, a lot of which are still sitting in suitcases, and she is keen to give them an airing. I have enjoyed sharing my house with Angel. Now the time is ripe for a change. We have survived living together for almost a year.

CHAPTER 37

It takes a few months for things to fall into place. Angel and Paulo's direction can change like the weather and there are shifts in their prospective landlord's plans. Dates are made and moved, but simply knowing that at some point they will be flying off to their love-nest means that listening to even their most crazed of confrontations is much easier.

Angel must really want this flat as she's been missing episodes of *The Jerry Springer Show* to work on her jewellery. For her that's dedication. What I am realising more and more is that Angel and Paulo enjoy it when they clash; it's a verbal form of jousting. In the open plan of a warehouse space they will be able to shout at each other over twelve hundred square feet, with no walls, doors or housemates to get in the way. I have a feeling they could both be very happy.

I escape sometimes to the peace of Matt's flat, though not too often. The benefit of a disastrous marriage is the opportunity to re-embrace the officially single state. I am wary of losing this bonus too quickly. It is pleasant and calm there, but I try not to let myself get into the habit of using it as a bolt-hole. Just the once he hints that he thinks that my casual approach to our friendship might be due to the more unusual contents of his wardrobe. This is not the case. If anything, the fact that we are still together so I can tease him about the length of time he takes to make up his face has a lot to do with what he is. I like him more for it, not less. I tell him as much but he still seems concerned.

'I don't know why I'm the way I am.'

'You don't need to. I don't know why I crave mint chocolate chip ice-cream but I'm not going to go into therapy for it,' I say as we lay curled in bed together, my clammy paw making its way downwards – to the part that gives him the most trouble when he wants to wear a tight lycra mini.

My friends (apart from Angel who is rather absorbed in her Burton–Taylor-style love affair) keep telling me I seem so happy. The effect of this is a bit like being told that I look ill or tired. I have that *do I?* air of puzzlement. I know that I'm definitely not unhappy, I just didn't realise that there are external signs. I have to study myself closely in the mirror to try and spot some of the symptoms.

As the date for Angel's move draws nearer, I try and make sure my general cheeriness is not too obvious. I don't want her to think that I am in high spirits due to her departure, as it is not so. Part of me is very sad to see her go. She is a unique ally and I am very grateful to the winds of fate for blowing her in my direction. I know my role as her friend, straight stooge and peacemaker is not over, only my role as a housemate. From her I have learned a few tricks of the trade when it comes to looking good, and just how far sheer verve can take you.

CHAPTER 38

Angel is jittery as the actual day for her relocation draws closer. She keeps coming into my room late at night to ask me whether she's doing the right thing. I try to be noncommittal. I would, if necessary, happily keep living with the pair of them and invest in heavy duty ear plugs but I won't take on the responsibility of making her decision.

I assure her that as I'm not ready for a new tenant yet, I'll keep her room empty just in case she ever wants to move back in a hurry. The night before she leaves we stay in to start the long process of getting all her things boxed up. More drinking and cackling than packing is carried out by the two of us. Angel is trying to persuade me that I want all the junk that she doesn't want to take with her.

'Go on, take it. I paid a fortune for that, it's Russian quartz,' she says, silkily brandishing a large light fitting. Her eyebrows tell me that she is lying through her teeth.

'It's plastic and it's broken – take it with you. I'm checking that none of this crap ends up mysteriously climbing out of their boxes in the night and being left behind.'

'This lovely pashmina scarf.'

'It's a raggedy old towel. Anyway, to quote you, "pashminas are *so* Nineties"!'

'You're so ungrateful. I offer you all these wonderful things and you throw them back in my face.'

'Hmm.' I'm unconvinced. With a friend like Angel you soon learn not to be too gullible.

'Okay, let's dump them,' she says reluctantly, finally acknowledging the fact that what she's been trying to off-load on me is mostly rubbish.

In the early hours of the morning we are already making drunken farewells before we say goodnight.

'It'll be strange not seeing your fuzzy little head in the morning,' Angel tells me affectionately.

'And I'm going to really miss removing matted clumps of hair from my bath plug,' I reply, feeling sad now that her departure is actually going to happen.

'I'm still going to make you come out with me all the time. It's not healthy to stay in too much – it drives you mad. You'll need to see me and down a bottle or five of wine every couple of days,' she says sternly, giving me a genuine bear hug, a rare commodity indeed from Angel.

'Of course I'll need regular doses of you to keep a little glamour in my life. Anyway, you're irreplaceable as a drinking partner, no one else I know can drink as heavily as you do. And don't worry about me being home alone. Haven't you noticed how sociable I've been of late? It'll be up to me to come and drag you out, to stop you sitting in front of the TV with Paulo and your dinner on a tray.'

That is about as emotional a farewell as either of us are capable of but it is an honest scene nevertheless. I will miss her, but we both realise that the beneficial nature of our partnership may have worked all the magic it was going to here in this small house. Our friendship will be firmly in place as she sets off with a new set of interior design dreams and her Brazilian lover.

I wake to the tune of Paulo and Angel arguing furiously about how many boxes a limousine can carry in one trip. I crawl back under the duvet blissful in the knowledge that it's not all my junk that has to be shifted. I will emerge from my bedroom only when the bulk of the vast job of moving Angel's stuff is nearly over and tempers have cooled down.

When I do emerge I am given the unenviable job of coaxing Angel's foul-breathed cat into one of those caged basket things. It skulks around at the back of the garden making sure there's always at least three feet between us. Eventually I manage to cage the beast and carry it yowling inside, trying to claw me through the bars.

I notice as I walk back to the house with the captive cat that my overgrown lawn is once again dotted with the white fluffy heads of dandelions nestling in the high grass. I am reminded of my childhood and of the secret hopes I used to set free while clutching a dandelion stalk.

Standing there lost in a daydream I'm struck by the pleasant feeling that I now have a new set of much bolder wishes for each puff of breath needed to set them all in flight.

Acknowledgements

Thanks to: Trudie Speke, my own bestower of blessings. Christina Drewett, for her angelic inspiration. My dear husband, for putting up with me with fortitude and patience.

Iron Shoes
Molly Giles

Kay Sorensen can't shake the feeling that she's 'stuck' in her life. She's a failed musician, disappointing daughter and resigned wife and mother. She envies her friend Zabeth – who seems to have the most vibrant sex life in the San Francisco Bay area – and the mysterious Charles Lichtman, with whom Kay feels destined to have an affair.

She has been unable to move out of the shadow of her glamorous and wickedly impossible mother, Ida. But now it seems that the illness Ida has almost revelled in is finally killing her. Having lived on courage, cigarettes and sarcasm for years, Ida still refuses to compromise. But, as infuriating as her mother can be, Kay is starting to realise that she is also the glue that holds their family together...

'storytelling at its best. Molly Giles's readers are blessed. Spread the word'   Amy Tan

'Giles gets inside her characters' heads, this touching novel will draw you in. Top read.'   *Company*

'wicked, affectionate, and amused. *Iron Shoes* can dance' Frances Mayes, author of *Under the Tuscan Sun* and *Bella Tuscany*

A SELECTION OF NOVELS AVAILABLE
FROM JUDY PIATKUS (PUBLISHERS) LIMITED

THE PRICES BELOW WERE CORRECT AT THE TIME OF GOING TO PRESS. HOWEVER, JUDY PIATKUS (PUBLISHERS) LIMITED RESERVE THE RIGHT TO SHOW NEW RETAIL PRICES ON COVERS WHICH MAY DIFFER FROM THOSE PREVIOUSLY ADVERTISED IN THE TEXT OR ELSEWHERE.

0 7499 3221 X	Iron Shoes	Molly Giles	£6.99
0 7499 3222 8	Persuading Annie	Melissa Nathan	£6.99
0 7499 3152 3	Pride, Prejudice & Jasmin Field	Melissa Nathan	£5.99
0 7499 3229 5	What If?	Shari Low	£5.99
0 7499 3212 0	Mad About The Girls	Francesca Clemintis	£5.99
0 7499 3143 4	Big Girls Don't Cry	Joanne Simms	£5.99

All Piatkus titles are available by post from:

Bookpost PLC, P.O. Box 29, Douglas, Isle of Man IM99 1BQ

Credit Cards accepted. Please telephone 01624 836000
Fax 01624 837033, Internet http://www.bookpost.co.uk
Or e-mail: bookshop@enterprise.net for details.

Free postage and packing in the UK. Overseas customers: allow £1 per book (paperbacks) and £3 per book (hardbacks).